Hannah keiyamason

CONVENT WALLS

Behind
CONVENT WALLS

by

Beth J. Coombe Harris

Reformation Heritage Books
Grand Rapids, Michigan

2006

Published by
Reformation Heritage Books
2965 Leonard St., NE
Grand Rapids, MI 49525
616-977-0599 / Fax 616-285-3246
e-mail: orders@heritagebooks.org
website: www.heritagebooks.org

originally published in London by Victory Press

10 digit ISBN 1-892777-96-7
13 digit ISBN 978-1-8927779-96-6

CONTENTS

FOREWORD

BY ENGINEER REAR-ADMIRAL ARCHIE R. EMDIN
C.M.G. (RETIRED)

OVER nineteen centuries have passed since Ovid said: " Ars est celare artem " ; and it is about one hundred years ago that Carlyle wrote; " Genius, which means transcendent capacity for taking trouble." Yet both of these sayings can well be written across the pages of this choice little book of our friend and neighbour, Miss Beth J. Coombe Harris, for, with patient discernment, she has delved into the dusty pages of French history, and, with artistic delicacy, she has drawn a vivid picture of some phases of those forgotten days that is both well timed and much needed.

For, in these latter days, much—if not all—of what Miss Harris herein writes about (whether in our own land or on the Continent) is so studiously excluded from the curriculum of our schools and universities that few—very few, alas! —recognise all that we owe to the great Protestant Reformation, nor do they realise the gross darkness from which our forefathers have rescued us, and that often at the cost of their own fortunes and lives. Quite recently, when talking to a friend—an evangelical lay-reader of the Church of England, and much used therein—about that old and excellent organisation, the Protestant Reformation Society, he asked, in all seriousness: " But why do Protestants need reforming ? "

The tale herein told centres about Charlotte de Bourbon, the girl-abbess of Jouarre, and later the devoted wife of William the Silent, Prince of Orange, from whom the present royal house of Great Britain traces its descent.[1]

It covers the early years of her eventful life, and a part of the internecine struggle between the Huguenots and the Romanists—and upon this solid, historic framework the authoress weaves the silver cords of natural love and human affection, with dainty touches of local colour, into a romance throbbing with life and vitality from which some very clear impressions emerge.

Firstly, and pre-eminently, the (to us) marvellous way in which God works out His own plan and purposes in grace, and what He achieves by His own Word, which truly does not return to Him void; but which, on the other hand does fully accomplish that which He pleases, and proves again, and yet again, that the Gospel of

[1] Louisa, daughter of Charlotte, Princess of Orange, became the wife of Frederick the Fourth, the Elector Palatine of the Rhine, and was the grandmother of Sophia, the Duchess of Brunswick, who was the mother of King George the First of England, whose grandson, the Duke of Kent, was the father of Queen Victoria, who was the great-grandmother of our present King.

Christ is the power of God unto salvation to every one that believeth.

Then, written in letters bold and large, one sees again the incalculable value and importance of early child training by a godly and devoted mother, and how the precious life-containing seed thus prayerfully sown and lovingly nurtured takes deep and abiding root, which subsequent earthly storms and trials can neither shake nor weaken. Who can say but what the faithful, loving Bible teaching of the child Charlotte by her saintly mother, Jaqueline, Duchess de Montpensier, is now bearing choice and precious fruit one hundredfold in what one so gladly learned, that our late most gracious sovereign, King George V, read a chapter of Holy Scripture every day, and that the Holy Bible was always on his table as the royal saloon train travelled from Euston to Balmoral !

Again, in this our loved and favoured land of freedom, we can probably never fully realise the absolutely unspeakable joy of those who suddenly find themselves for the first time in possession of a whole Bible of their very own, and—what is even more—liberty to read it, when the way of salvation had previously only been made known by scattered passages of Scripture received at broken intervals by stealth, and often at the risk of life itself.

So, for its timely message, its intrinsic value, and its literary merits, this book is warmly commended; and with the earnest hope that, like its predecessor, *Gillian's Treasure*, it may also be used of God to the enlightening of precious souls into the liberty wherewith Christ has made us free.

Heathfield.

INTRODUCTION

THE main facts in the life of Charlotte de
Bourbon told in this story are authentic: her
early training; the diverse religious opinions of
her parents; her mother's prediction; her position
in the convent and subsequently in the world.

The historical characters named are:

The Duke and Duchess de Montpensier and
their daughters.

Cousin Jeanne.

Henri Robert de la Marke, Duke de Bouillon.

Elizabeth, Queen of England.

Henry, King of France.

Charles, King of France, his nurse, and his
surgeon.

Catharine de Medici.

William, Prince of Orange, his wives and
daughters.

Admiral Coligny.

M. Teligny.

The President of the French Parliament.

The Elector Palatine.

Prince of Condé.

Duke of Anjou.

Maréchal de Retz.

Duke de Guise.

All other characters are fictitious.

CHAPTER I

A FATHER'S DECREE

THREE children were playing merrily together in an old-world garden in France about the year 1557.

On the terrace of the château, Louis de Bourbon, the Duke de Montpensier, a prince of the royal blood of France, and his wife, Jaqueline, stood together watching the children. On the face of the Duchess a gentle smile played, but the Duke's face was gloomy.

The three children were Charlotte de Bourbon, tall for her ten years and graceful in all her movements; Henri de Valois, a high-spirited boy of eight; and wee Yvonne d'Arande, a curly-headed, fragile-looking child of seven. Before long they were joined by a nurse bearing in her arms a baby—the little sister of Henri.

With a cry of delight Charlotte ran to meet the nurse, exclaiming: " May I hold the darling ? Do, do let me, please ! "

The nurse, with a smile, seated herself on a rustic bench beneath a spreading tree, and Charlotte was allowed to sit beside her and have the baby on her lap.

Henri and Yvonne continued playing with their ball, and Henri called: " Charlotte, don't waste your time with the baby. Come and play."

But Charlotte shook her head.

" I can't. I love babies and I never hardly get

one to nurse. Isn't she just perfect ? " she continued, turning to the nurse.

Meanwhile the Duchess, noticing her daughter's delight with the baby, remarked: "What an ideal mother Charlotte will make when she is grown up."

" Don't talk nonsense, Jaqueline," the Duke replied, a stern note in his tone. " I have other plans for Charlotte. You may as well make up your mind to that at once. Charlotte will enter that convent at Jouarre before long. I am fully determined on this, so it will be useless for you to remonstrate."

" Oh, Louis," the Duchess exclaimed, " I must, I must protest. Already you have taken Louise and Jeanne from me and placed them in convents. Frances is married, and I did think you would let me plan as I wish for my little Charlotte."

" Well, I suppose you do not wish to complain because your eldest daughter is married. The Duke de Bouillon makes her a good husband."

" Oh yes, I know that. But it is Charlotte for whom I plead. Husband, it was not long ago that you spoke of betrothing her to the son of our friend the Duke de Longueville. Why have you given up that idea ? "

" For a great many reasons, Madame. First, because of the impoverished condition of my estates: heavy taxation is ruining me, and I do not feel inclined to make an effort to find a suitable dowry for Charlotte. Secondly, I know you are doing your best to make the child a Protestant, and I am determined she shall be a Roman Catholic. Thirdly, what could be better for us when we die than to have three daughters living cloistered lives, and so able to devote their energies to praying for our souls that we may be released from purgatory ? "

The Duchess's face was tense with emotion, but she strove to speak quietly.

" Louis, my husband, would that you believed as I do, that a simple faith in the finished work of Christ for forgiveness and salvation is what is needed for our future. The Holy Book does not speak of purgatory, and——"

" Peace, woman." The Duke interrupted his wife angrily. " I will not listen to such heresy. Do you wish to bring upon us the wrath of the priests ? Are you not aware of the hatred of the King against Protestants ? Believe me, a time is coming before long when the fact that you are the wife of a man faithful to the Romish Church will not be sufficient to protect you from the punishment you doubtless merit."

" But, Louis," the Duchess spoke again, " this is news to me. Has not Henri our King been tolerant to Protestants ? Why, in Paris a Huguenot church has been recently erected, and persons of distinction are adherents of the reformed faith. I heard only a short time ago that there are four hundred thousand in our land who worship God according to the teaching of the Bible."

" That may be so, but I have reliable information that things will be otherwise before many years have passed. Our King has been absorbed in war with Spain, but now he is turning his attention to matters of religion in the kingdom, and these wretched heretics will be brought to book. Besides which, every one knows on which side the Queen is. Catharine de Medici will use all her influence to forward the suppression of Protestantism. So, beware ! If you value your child's life, teach her obedience to the priests."

So saying, the Duke de Montpensier turned away, and his wife entered the château, her face clouded with anxiety.

Reaching her boudoir, she flung herself on her knees and prayed.

Powerless as she was to protect her little daughter, futile as she knew it was to argue with her imperious husband, she found her refuge and solace in pouring out her heart to the Heavenly Father, whose power to save and help was as in the days of old, of which she read with delight in her Bible.

Jaqueline, Duchess de Montpensier, was a simple, Protestant Christian. She possessed a Bible and Calvin's book, *Christian Institutes*, which was a compendium of the elementary principles of true religion. With these two books the Duchess spent much time, and, taught by the Holy Spirit, without human instruction, she sought to win others for Christ.

Frances, her eldest daughter, was one with her mother in the faith, and the Duchess missed her sorely when she left her home on the occasion of her marriage. Now, as the Duchess in her sorrow knelt by her couch, she prayed earnestly for little Charlotte, her tears flowed and her requests were fragmentary. However, after a time she grew calm, and a strong conviction came to her that, even if Charlotte entered a convent, compelled by her father, yet somehow, some time, God would release her, and she would become a happy wife and mother. It seemed, humanly speaking, an absolute impossibility. If once Charlotte became a nun, the vows which she would be compelled to take would be considered irrevocable, and escape from the cloistered life and a return to ordinary circumstances not to be considered for a moment. Yet, in spite of all that there was against it, the Duchess felt a calm conviction that all would be well for her child. Quietly and confidently she commended Charlotte to God's keeping, and then rose from her knees.

Just at that moment a slight noise at her door attracted her attention; a small scratching sound, which she knew meant that someone sought admittance. In those days a slight scratch on the door, not a knock, was the sign that someone was waiting to enter.

"Come hither," the Duchess called, and Charlotte entered, making a deep curtsey.

The Duchess saw by the eager look in Charlotte's eyes that some request was about to be made, and she smiled as she asked: "What is it you want, my child?"

"Oh, Madame, nurse says Henri must go home now, and Yvonne's nurse has come for her, so they both have to go, but they want to know if they may come to-morrow to hear one of your stories."

"Yes, certainly. I shall be delighted to tell you all a story to-morrow morning."

Charlotte expressed her thanks and quickly disappeared into the garden to tell Henri and Yvonne to come again on the morrow.

CHAPTER II

LITTLE Yvonne d'Arande was a lonely child, a pathetic, small maiden with a wistful, apprehensive look in her big brown eyes. Her mother had died when the child was three years old. Yvonne's experience of life had taught her to fear all grown-up people with the exception of the Duchess de Montpensier. In her own home she always had the uneasy sensation that those in authority were liable at any time, and without —as far as she could tell—any reason, to fall upon her with dire threats of vengeance, and not only threats, but painful actualities.

Yvonne's recollection of her mother was but faint, but she cherished the memory of a gracious personality in whose presence she had been happy and secure, someone who had loved her. Dimly she could recall a scene in which she had taken part: a shadowed room with curtains screening the summer sunshine; a big bed wherein, on many pillows, rested the face she loved; and of herself being lifted on to the bed to be held in her mother's grasp and kissed, while that gentle voice she was to hear no more exclaimed: " My baby ! Oh, my baby ! "

Yvonne was sure she remembered that, but when she had spoken of it to her governess, that lady replied: " Nonsense, child. You were only three when your mother died. You've got too much imagination."

So Yvonne spoke of it no more, but nevertheless she pondered on it and whispered to herself: "Somebody loved me once."

Of her father Yvonne knew little. He was seldom at home, and when, on his infrequent and brief visits, she was brought into his presence she was dumb with shyness, and he thought her a stupid, uninteresting child, albeit a pretty one. Could he have seen her playing with her little neighbour, Henri, or listening with rapt attention to the Duchess, he would have been obliged to have changed his opinion, for vivacity and intelligence were writ large on the child's countenance.

Yvonne's greatest joy was to visit Charlotte de Bourbon's home, and, when Charlotte's mother gathered the little ones round her and told them stories of the One who loved the children, Yvonne's heart opened to receive the good news, like a wee flower opening its petals in the spring sunshine.

Yvonne's nurse did occasionally consent to taking the child to the château of the de Bourbons, for, while Yvonne played with Charlotte or listened to the Duchess, she was free to enjoy a gossip with the servants of the castle. So, when Yvonne timidly asked—on the morning of the next day after the Duke had told his wife of his intentions concerning Charlotte—if she might go to visit Charlotte, nurse consented; and presently Charlotte, Yvonne, and Henri gathered in the Duchess's sitting-room ready to listen to the promised story.

" May we not be on the terrace, Madame ? "
Charlotte asked. " It is such a lovely morning."

She was surprised at her mother's decided
" No," for she did not understand that the
Duchess was anxious that no one should overhear
her as she talked to the children. She realised
that at any time her husband might put a stop
to these little gatherings. There were spies in
her home, and her husband's chaplain—one in
religious views with his employer—might be
hovering round unseen, but with ears keen to
catch her every word, were they in the open.
So, with doors carefully closed, the Duchess read
to the children the story of Samuel.

" Only a little boy," she said, as she finished
the Bible reading; " and yet he heard God's Voice,
and he belonged to God and served Him."

Charlotte's eyes were roving—her attention
was caught by a bee buzzing in the window—but
Yvonne's face was flushed with interest, and her
eyes were shining.

" Could a little girl belong to God and hear
His Voice, or is it only boys ? " she asked.

The Duchess's smile was very tender. She put
her arm round the little questioner and said:
" God wants the little girls as well as the boys.
God loves you, little one, and you can belong to
Him and serve Him."

" Nurse says nobody loves me. I'm not very
good."

" Yvonne," the Duchess spoke slowly and impressively, " I want you to remember always that
God loves you."

" I'm so glad," Yvonne said simply. " I'm so

glad God loves me, and I'd like to belong to Him now."

Henri grew a little tired of Yvonne absorbing the Duchess's attention, and he broke in:

" God loves me too, doesn't He ? Wouldn't He like another boy to serve Him now that Samuel is dead ? "

" Yes, indeed, Henri. You can come to Him now. And remember, wherever you are, you can always come to God and tell Him everything; when you are away from friends, and there seems no one to help you, God can and will, if you ask Him."

Charlotte and Henri were showing signs of restlessness, and the Duchess said: " You can all go into the pleasance now, and have a game."

Charlotte and Henri readily availed themselves of the permission, but Yvonne lingered.

" May I stay with you a little longer ? " she asked.

The Duchess said nothing, but she lifted the child on her lap, and Yvonne's slight little form nestled in her friend's arms with a sigh of contentment.

" Do tell me another story, please," she said.

The Duchess could not have explained why, but somehow, at that moment, she had a sense that the present opportunity of talking to the child was priceless; a vague feeling took possession of her that this was to be the last time she would have the chance of giving the little one teaching that would be a help to her for many months, or, maybe, years to come. So she lifted her heart to God for guidance as to which Bible story she should relate, and her mind was directed to the Old Testament account of the three men in the burning, fiery furnace.

Yvonne listened breathlessly as the Duchess told her of the powerful king who made a great image and commanded all his subjects to fall down and worship the image at the moment when the band should burst into music.

" Three men refused to do this," said the Duchess, " for they knew they must worship God only, not an image, and they loved God too much to do anything that would grieve Him. The king was exceedingly angry and commanded that these three men should be thrown into a furnace, where a big fire was burnnig, for the king meant them to be killed. But a lovely thing happened. The king looked and saw, not three men, but four, walking unhurt amid the flames, and the king recognised that the fourth Man was the Son of God."

Yvonne sat upright and, with flushed face, said: " Was it really Jesus ? "

" Yes," the Duchess replied. " And, Yvonne, Jesus is always with those who suffer for His sake. He never, never forsakes those who love Him."

" I think," said Yvonne, slowly and thoughtfully, " those men must have been very happy in that burning, fiery furnace with Jesus so close to them. Don't you ? "

" Yes, dear heart, I do. Jesus can make us happy wherever we are. Supposing, Yvonne, you had a big trouble. If I came to see you, would you tell me about it ? "

" Yes, I would," Yvonne replied.

" I want you to remember that, if you are somewhere far away from friends, yet you may tell
Jesus everything. Just speak straight to Him,
and tell Him just as you would tell me. He can
always hear you, and you need not pray to the
Virgin Mary or to the saints. Jesus died on the
Cross for you, to open up the way to God for all,
so we may come freely to Him."

" Nurse says I must pray to Saint Barbara,
but I like telling Jesus things best," Yvonne said
simply.

" I am so glad you do, dear," the Duchess
responded.

" And what happened to the men in the
furnace after that ? " Yvonne asked, and the
Duchess told her of their deliverance and how
the king himself worshipped God.

The conversation sank into little Yvonne's
heart, and in the sad days so soon to come in her
life she never forgot the story she had heard that
morning, and many times the memory brought
comfort to her heart.

The Duchess watched the child depart with
her nurse, and again a strange foreboding filled
her mind that some untoward circumstance
would arise which would prevent the opportunity
occurring again of telling Yvonne more of the
Saviour. She felt sad, but yet thankful that a
seed had been sown in that little heart, and, with
a prayer that God would watch over the seed
and bring it to fruition, she turned to other work.

Meanwhile Yvonne ran along beside her nurse
quite content, hugging her big doll, her greatest

treasure. It was made of wood and was practically indestructible, hard and unyielding, but Yvonne's imaginative mind endued it with marvellous understanding. To her doll—Suzanne by name —she told all her troubles and was convinced that Suzanne sympathised. Every night she fell asleep with Suzanne held tight, and poor little Yvonne, having no other outlet for her love in her home, poured out a pathetic offering at the shrine of the unconscious, indifferent Suzanne.

Not many days after this the Duke came into the Duchess's boudoir with the astonishing news that Yvonne's father had been killed—thrown from his horse—and death had been instantaneous.

" Oh, poor little Yvonne," the Duchess exclaimed. " Poor wee child ! What will become of her, left an orphan ? She has no near relations."

" No, and her father's affairs are in a shocking condition, I understand. He has let things gc to pieces since his wife's death. An elderly cousin and his wife have arrived, and the plan is to put Yvonne into a convent. After d'Arande's debts are paid there won't be a great deal left. What there is will be paid over to the convent authorities as compensation for taking the child."

The Duchess sat silent for a few moments, then she said timidly: " Louis, I suppose it is useless for me to suggest our having the child here. I would willingly undertake the care of her. She can be educated with Charlotte. The expense would be but trifling."

The Duke frowned heavily.

"Nonsense, Jaqueline. I know what your idea is: to bring up the child to be a Protestant.

No, no; let her be under the care of those who will see she becomes a good Catholic. I wouldn't lift a finger to assist in making a heretic of her. Her parents' faith is the right one for the child."

" Her parents ! " echoed the Duchess. "I doubt if her mother was a Roman Catholic, and her poor father had no religion."

" Nonsense," again said the Duke. " Her mother was buried with the rites of the true Church. That is sufficient."

The Duchess lost no time in visiting Yvonne's home, but the cousin's wife, a stern-faced, middle-aged woman, gave the Duchess no opportunity of seeing the child alone. So she could only whisper, in saying farewell: " God will take care of you, dear heart."

It seemed that all concerned were determined that Yvonne should be—as they termed it—" Dedicated to Holy Mother Church." And the Duchess left, sad at heart, while Yvonne's relations congratulated themselves that they were acquiring merit by giving to God something for which they had no use for themselves. In fact they thought it a highly desirable thing to have a young relative devoted to religion; it cast a shadow of reflected sanctity on them, and would she not be able to pray for their souls at great length when the time came—long may it be delayed—that they should have passed from this world into the great beyond ?

It was a chilly, uncomfortable morning when the big, unwieldy carriage, formerly owned by M. d'Arande, Yvonne's father, rumbled out of the grounds of the only home Yvonne had ever known.

Inside the coach were seated Yvonne—grasping tightly her loved Suzanne—and Yvonne's cousin's wife, Madame de Palissier.

Yvonne's little face was white and anxious. Unpleasant as life had been for her in her father's château, yet she would rather have continued with the ills she knew than face possible ills to which at present she was a stranger, for now she was being conveyed to the convent to be left to the care of strangers, and Yvonne's experience of life gave her little hope of finding love and tenderness in the future.

Silently she sat perched on her seat, gazing wistfully through the window. Suddenly she sprang to her feet and called: " Gaspar, Gaspar, stop ! I must speak to Henri." For she had caught sight of Henri walking with his tutor.

Madame de Palissier put a restraining hand on her and called: " Certainly not, Gaspar. Proceed on the journey."

But old Gaspar the coachman was slightly deaf, and could be very deaf if he so wished. Now he chose only to hear his little mistress's cry, and checked his horses as he drew near Henri.

" Henri, Henri ! " Yvonne called. " They're taking me to a convent. Oh, Henri ! "

Henri sprang on to the step of the coach and exclaimed: " Too bad, Yvonne ! Never mind, as soon as I'm old enough I'll come and get you out. Just wait till I'm a man ! "

" Oh, will you really, Henri ? " Yvonne's face

brightened. " Promise me, promise, Henri."

" I do," the boy spoke seriously.

Henri's tutor now joined him, and, seeing the annoyed look on Madame de Palissier's face, he bade Henri come away.

So, with a hasty " Good-bye," Henri got down from the carriage-step and followed his tutor, who remarked: " Going to be a knight-errant, are you, and rescue imprisoned damsels, eh ? "

" No. Only one. And that will be Yvonne. It's a shame shutting her up like that," Henri said sturdily.

Meanwhile the coach rolled on, and Madame de Palissier took the opportunity of speaking seriously to Yvonne about her future.

Madame was remembering uneasily that escape from a convent was not altogether an impossibility. True, it was exceedingly unusual, but she recalled how, thirty-four years before, in 1523, a party of nuns led by Katherine von Bora, who afterwards became Martin Luther's wife, had escaped from a convent. Certainly that was in Germany and this was France; but what had been done might be accomplished again, so she there and then set to work to guide the youthful mind of little Yvonne into what Madame considered a right line of thought.

" Yvonne," she said, " listen to me. You must not think anything more of what that silly boy promised. You are going to live always in the convent. It will be a beautiful life for you, and when you are older and can then take your vows you will be the ' bride of Heaven ' and God will be very pleased with you."

" Will He ? " Yvonne said doubtfully.

" Yes, indeed. We people that are in the world cannot please Him, but you will as you pray and sing and—— "

The good lady broke off. She was about to add " fast," but thought it wiser not.

Possibly Yvonne would not have understood her, but she was an intelligent child, and she said: " I'm sure God is pleased with the Duchess, and she's not in a convent."

Madame de Palissier's temper was short, so she replied sharply: " Don't talk nonsense. Remember, you are to forget that boy entirely. You will never, never see him again. What you have to do now is to be a good girl and do exactly what the nuns tell you. Now, don't talk to me. I want to be quiet."

CHAPTER III

A BURNING, FIERY FURNACE

THE arrival of Yvonne at the convent was almost unnoticed by the inmates. Except for the fact that she was younger than most new-comers, her advent was of no importance. She had no influential friends nor was she wealthy. Had it been Charlotte de Bourbon who had entered that monastic establishment it would have been far otherwise, for Charlotte's father, the Duke de Montpensier, was of illustrious rank and possessed great influence, both at the royal court and with ecclesiastical authorities; in fact, it was rumoured that on the death of the abbess then in power at the convent of Jouarre, the Duke had the means of pulling strings which would result in his naming her successor.

Yvonne was pleased to find in her new home there were girls only a few years older than herself, and there seemed a fair prospect of her settling in happily. All the young people were kept busy. Lessons, very especially in embroidery and fine needlework, alternated with church services and work in the still-room, where medicines of all sorts were concocted, also pleasant drinks, preserves, sweetmeats, toilet requisites, and many other things.

Yvonne liked her lessons, but her fragile little body grew weary when kneeling for a long period on the cold stone floor of the church listening to the monotonous repetition of Latin prayers offered to the Virgin Mary and various saints. It was some time before Yvonne realised to whom the prayers were addressed. When it dawned upon her, she recalled distinctly the words of the Duchess: " You need not pray to the Virgin Mary or to the saints. Jesus died on the Cross to open up the way to God for us, so come straight to Him." And often and often Yvonne whispered her own simple petitions to God in the name of the Lord Jesus.

Life went on quietly for some months. Yvonne was gentle and obedient, very retiring in disposition. She spent her time of recreation each day in playing with her much-loved Suzanne, and the other girls, all being older, left her largely to herself. It seemed that Yvonne was not likely to attract much attention, until one day one of the girls fell ill. She was a big girl of fourteen years and rather a favourite with the others. At recreation time this illness was being discussed, and some of the girls gloomily prophesied that Madeline—the sick girl—would not recover.

Yvonne listening, suddenly said: " We could ask Jesus to make her well."

It was unusual for Yvonne to volunteer a remark; she seldom spoke except in answer to some question, and the girls were surprised.

One said: " I offered a prayer to Saint Anne this morning for Madeline."

Again Yvonne spoke, not realising in her innocence what a storm she would arouse. " We need not pray to a saint. The Duchess told me to pray straight to God, in the Name of Jesus.

Jesus said: ' Let the little children come unto Me.' "

There was a moment of awe-struck silence, then one girl spoke.

" You little heretic ! Whatever will Sister Marie Thérèse say to you ? She hates heretics, and so does the Abbess. You'll have to be taught better, that's for certain."

" Shall you tell ? " queried another.

" No, don't," said a third. " Don't get the poor babe into trouble."

But the first speaker's lips set firmly with a grim look of determination, and after a pause she said: " I consider it my duty to tell. If you allow evil in our midst unchecked it may spread. I shall certainly speak to Sister Marie Thérèse. She will know what to do."

The bell for lessons rang then, and the girls trooped into the schoolroom, Yvonne feeling a little bewildered as to what these bigger girls meant.

She was not left long in doubt. Sister Marie Thérèse was made acquainted with what had taken place, and soon she drew the attention of the Abbess to Yvonne and her religious views.

The Abbess had no hesitation in deciding that such ideas must be eradicated from the child's memory without delay, and sent Sister Marie Thérèse to fetch her.

Yvonne had never been in the Abbess's room before, and she felt shy and frightened. The Abbess sat in her high-backed chair, a tall, attenuated figure with colourless face, thin lips, sharp hard eyes, and gnarled hands. She seemed to little Yvonne an awe-inspiring personality indeed.

However, the Abbess spoke quietly to the child as she stood in front of her with hands placed behind her.

" Yvonne," the old lady said, " I want you to tell me what the Duchess de Montpensier taught you about our blessed Virgin's Son."

Here she and Sister Marie Thérèse, who stood behind the Abbess's chair, crossed themselves.

Yvonne looked puzzled, and, after a pause, she said: " I don't think she told me anything about Him."

The Abbess turned to Sister Marie Thérèse. " I thought you said—— "

Sister Marie Thérèse forgot her manners and interrupted, speaking sharply to Yvonne.

" Don't tell lies, you naughty child. I heard you say the other day that the Duchess taught you about Jesus."

" Oh-h ! " Yvonne's face cleared. " I didn't know you meant Jesus who loves the little children."

Yvonne became enthusiastic at once, and promptly began to tell some of the beautiful truths which she had learned from the Duchess.

The Abbess frowned, and, after listening a little while, said: " That will do, child. Now I want you to understand that in the future you must address your prayers to the Virgin Mary, the blessed Mother of God. It is very "—she paused for a word suitable to the understanding of a child—" bold of you to speak to the Lord Jesus. You must promise me never to do that again

c

or I shall have to punish you severely."

Yvonne's little face, a moment before so animated, as she spoke of the Saviour she loved, grew clouded, but she answered with a firmness that amazed her listeners. " I can't promise. I always tell Jesus everything. The Duchess said I could, and I do."

The Abbess's temper was quickly roused. Absolutely monarch in her little kingdom, imperious to a degree, she was exceedingly angry that this small child should refuse to comply with her wishes, and to quote the authority of a woman of the world. The Duchess, indeed ! Who was she in comparison with one who held so high an office in the Church ?

She sat still a moment meditating as to what suitable punishment she should inflict on Yvonne. There was very little that happened in that building but what those keen eyes noticed, and the Abbess had not failed to note the devotion which Yvonne gave to her doll Suzanne. The memory of it came to the old lady's mind as she sat there contemplating Yvonne and her rebellion, and, turning to Sister Marie Thérèse, she said: " Bring the child's doll here."

Wonderingly Sister Marie Thérèse obeyed, and in a few minutes returned, bearing Yvonne's treasure. The Abbess took it, and, turning to Yvonne, said: " Now once again I ask you, will you do as I bid you, and in future address your prayer to the Virgin Mary ? Or—let me see— to-day is the sixteenth of December, Saint Barbara's day, and she shall be your patron saint. She was a very virtuous woman and is able to protect all who pray to her, especially those in danger in time of thunderstorms. Sister Marie Thérèse shall tell you her story and teach you a little prayer. Now promise me you will do as I say."

Yvonne's eyes filled with tears as she tremblingly answered: " I must speak to Jesus. He loves me and comforts me, and if I promised not to, I know I should still do it. The Duchess said—— "

" That's enough ! " the Abbess said. " Then you must take your punishment."

There was a large fire burning on the hearth, and the Abbess passed Suzanne to Sister Marie Thérèse with the words: " Put the doll on the fire."

Sister Marie Thérèse promptly obeyed. With a scream Yvonne sprang to the hearth, and would have plunged her hands into the flames to rescue her treasure, but the Abbess laid firm hands on the child's shoulders and held her in front of the fire, in order that she might watch the cremation of her Suzanne.

To Yvonne it was a moment of agony. So long had she credited Suzanne with the qualities of humanity that she had no doubt that her doll felt those scorching, leaping flames. In terror-stricken silence she watched until Suzanne fell to pieces in a red-grey heap, then Yvonne crumpled up in the Abbess's hands, in a faint.

" Call Sister Marie Gabrielle," said the Abbess briefly, and presently there arrived the infirmarian, the old nun who took charge of all sick folk in the convent. Sister Marie Gabrielle was getting aged, but was still vigorous. All her life, since she entered the convent at the age of sixteen, she had studied healing arts and practised them for many long years. Her herb garden in the convent precincts was known for miles around, and the peasants frequently visited the convent when suffering, to obtain Sister Marie Gabrielle's aid.

She was never happier than when some helpless one looked to her for relief, and she had great success in her ministrations.

Now, with a reproachful glance at the two women, she picked up the unconscious little form and bore Yvonne off to the infirmary, where she—as infirmarian—had complete control.

It was some time before Yvonne revived, and then only to lie white and dumb on the bed where she had been placed.

" Leave her alone," Sister Marie Gabrielle counselled her helpers. " She has had a shock, and restoration will take time." But as the days passed and still Yvonne showed no signs of recovery, even old Sister Marie Gabrielle began to feel alarmed. The child never spoke aloud, but sometimes her lips moved; and, bending over her one day, Sister Marie Gabrielle caught the words: " A burning, fiery furnace."

" Poor lamb ! Don't think about that. Sister will get you a new doll."

The story of Suzanne's fate had reached Sister Marie Gabrielle's ears, and she had the clue to Yvonne's suffering condition.

The child shook her head mournfully. No other doll could ever take Suzanne's place. Then suddenly she sat up in bed, exclaiming: " Oh, I forgot ! Jesus was with them in the burning, fiery furnace, and He comforted them. He will comfort me. The Duchess said He would."

From that moment Yvonne began to recover, but it was slow work, and Sister Marie Gabrielle took care that it should not be hastened unduly. As long as possible she kept Yvonne under her care, and the child learnt to love the old nun very dearly.

" When I'm big enough," she asked, " may I be your helper and learn to make medicines like Sister Marie Cécile does ? "

" I'll see if the Abbess will let you begin now. There's lots you could do in the garden to save me from stooping," Sister Marie Gabrielle replied.

At her first opportunity Sister Marie Gabrielle had a few words with the Abbess. The Abbess inquired how the obstinate child was progressing, and added: " I've not done with her yet."

" You'll be wise to leave the child alone. You don't want an idiot on your hands. Another shock like that last and the child's brain will give way. In time, the memory of the teaching she has had will fade, without harsh treatment."

Sister Marie Gabrielle was the only one who ventured to speak her mind to the Abbess, but long years before either of them had entered upon a cloistered life they had been friends, and Sister Marie Gabrielle had always kept to her privilege as a friend, of expressing her opinion.

So now the Abbess replied: " Have it your own way, but keep the child out of my sight."

So Yvonne did fewer lessons, and spent much time in the garden with Sister Marie Gabrielle; and so happier days dawned, and she grew rosy and strong.

God had watched over her, and, even in the midst of foes, had been with her, comforting and caring for the little one.

CHAPTER IV

CHARLOTTE'S REBELLION

CHARLOTTE DE BOURBON, unconscious of the plans being made for her future by her father, lived her happy, care-free life in the old château. She loved both her parents, but her deepest devotion was for her mother; consequently, as the heart so often dominates the mind, Charlotte was more inclined to believe the teaching given her by the Duchess than to pay much heed to the lectures on religion given her by her father and her father's chaplain.

The Duke, feeling that the time was drawing near when Charlotte should be sent to the convent of his choice, consulted with the chaplain, Father Anselme, as to the best way of preparing her for the change. He shrank from the task himself, for, determined as he was on this course of action, he anticipated opposition from his little daughter, who inherited her father's strong will. Moreover, he was fond of the child in his own fashion; underneath the heavy crust of bigotry, superstition, and self-will there was a father's heart.

Father Anselme readily undertook to talk to Charlotte at her next lesson-hour. Charlotte seated herself complacently in the library and prepared to repeat her task, but Father Anselme checked her and said in his suave voice: " My child, I have much to say to you this morning, and I want you to give careful heed to my speech."

Then he proceeded to tell her some legends of the saints: how they had, one and all, renounced the world, chosen, as a higher and more attractive life, to retire to monastery or convent and live a life of meditation and piety.

" Think you, my daughter, of the joys of such a surrender," he continued. " This girl of whom I have been telling you became the bride of Heaven; she became an exalted being, honoured by all who knew her, and is now worshipped by many. She was no older than you when she heard the call. My child, do you not hear a voice speaking to you ? Calling—— "

" No, I don't, and I don't want to," Charlotte interrupted.

" But you wish to be a good and holy woman, don't you ? "

" I want to be like Mother. She is a good woman, and she's not a nun, and I'm not going to be. I'm going to marry and—— "

It was the priest who interrupted this time. " Hush, my child. You do not—— "

" I'm not going to hush. I tell you I'm not going to be a nun, and I think that girl you were talking about was very silly, and all others who go into convents are, too, when they might be just as good in their own homes. You know, Father took me to see Cousin Jeanne, and I made up my mind then, when I saw her in that horrid, woollen frock and heavy veil, and shut in like she was. I simply won't be a nun."

Father Anselme rose.

" Come with me," he said. " I must punish you for your rebellious words. Silent meditation may bring you to a better frame of mind."

Charlotte dared not refuse to follow him. She was feeling somewhat alarmed at her daring in answering as she had done, but said she to herself: " I must make it plain at once that I don't intend to be a nun, or they may fix me up, before I know what they are about."

Father Anselme led the way to the chapel, Charlotte following.

" Now, my daughter," he said, " you will lie here on the cold floor prostrate before this crucifix until vespers. Meditate on what I have told you of the high calling which is yours; of the opportunity you will have for prayer; of the office to which you may attain in time—for, with your father's influence, doubtless you will be at an early age appointed to the exalted position of an abbess. Remember that in the office of the Holy Church, no worldly rank could ever be so great, so important, as yours, if you become the head of an order. And, as you give yourself to meditation, to worship, in time you may become a saint, and your name go down to posterity, even as the one of whom I was telling you."

Father Anselme waited to see that Charlotte obeyed him, stretching herself on the tessellated floor. It was only ten o'clock in the morning, and the prospect of lying there all day did not please Charlotte; but, with her usual sang-froid, she determined to make the best of it. No sooner had the echo of the priest's step died away than she sprang to her feet and quickly collected cushions from the pews, and proceeded to make for herself a cosy nest. Later in the day, when Father Anselme came to see if the silence of the chapel and the long prostration had, as he hoped, subdued her turbulent spirit, he found Charlotte comfortably and soundly asleep.

When Father Anselme, with much indignation, reported this to the Duke, he laughed heartily.

" Charlotte will never be given to mortifying the flesh, I fancy. Nevertheless," he added, his face growing grave, " my purpose knows no change. To Jouarre she will go within a year or two, so continue to do your best to reconcile her to her fate, Father. I am in communication with the Abbess there, and she holds herself in readiness to receive Charlotte at any time."

" She should consider it high honour to receive the daughter of the Duke de Montpensier," he replied, " as doubtless she does."

The Duke smiled. Father Anselme knew how to please his patron.

" Is not that child, Yvonne d'Arande there ? How does she fare ? " the priest continued.

" Oh, a troublesome child, I gathered from the Abbess when I inquired. Holds, even at her tender age, heretical views; but that nonsense will get knocked out of her as she gets older."

A shrewd look spread over the priest's face as he queried: " Where did the child imbibe the ideas ? Not in her father's home, I fancy."

The Duke frowned heavily. He knew whence Yvonne had learnt Reformation truths, and he knew that Father Anselme knew, and meant it to be a reminder to him of his wife's attitude toward Roman Catholicism and a warning that Charlotte was getting the same teaching.

He grew angry and exclaimed: " Look here, Father, if you can't counteract the teaching of a woman, what's the use of my maintaining you here. Surely, with your knowledge and the authority I give you over Charlotte, you ought to be able to lay a solid foundation of submission, and so present the desirability of convent life to her that, when the time comes for her removal from home, she may go with willingness. I don't want a fuss."

The priest knew his place, and he remarked humbly: " Give me time, sir, and I shall doubtless succeed."

The Duke left him, and the priest stood in silent thought. He had spoken hopefully, but in reality he doubted whether he should ever persuade high-spirited Charlotte to accept willingly the life planned for her.

Charlotte and Henri, still good friends, did not forget their erstwhile little playmate, Yvonne. They missed her, and Charlotte mournfully remarked: " We shall never see her again, Henri. How I hate those horrid old convents. They're just prisons."

" We *shall* see her again, Charlotte." Henri spoke with a note of decision in his tone, unusual in a boy of his age. " I promised Yvonne when I said good-bye to her that I would rescue her when I am a man—and so I will."

" You don't know what you're talking about,

Henri. I went to see Cousin Jeanne in her convent. There were high walls and such heavy doors, and even when Mother and I were taken inside we only saw Cousin Jeanne on the other side of a sort of a window, just an opening with bars. You'll never get in to Yvonne, leave alone getting her out." Charlotte spoke gravely. Henri, too, was serious, and he stood silent for a few moments. Then he said: " I tell you what, Charlotte. You know what the Duchess told us about Peter in prison, and how God got him out; well, I'm going to ask God to show me how to get Yvonne out some day, and I believe He will."

Charlotte sighed. Henri and Yvonne both seemed to have grasped her mother's teaching better than she had done.

" Oh, I don't know," she said at length. " One thing I know—I don't want to get inside a convent myself. Father says I shall have to when I am older, and I don't see how I'm to prevent him sending me."

" Can't the Duchess say she won't let you go," Henri suggested.

Charlotte shook her head mournfully and said with keen intuition: " If Mother said that it would only make Father more determined than ever. He is always so contrary with Mother. But there, don't let us bother about it to-day. Come to the stables with me and see Bobette's puppies—they're just delicious." And soon the two children were laughing merrily over the queer antics of the five delightful, plump, white ınd black puppies crawling over one another and basking in the sunshine of the stable-yard.

For the time being all serious matters were forgotten.

CHAPTER V

THE HERB GARDEN

IF Charlotte and Henri sometimes thought of Yvonne, they were remembered every day by Yvonne in her prison. She was a faithful little soul, and constantly she thought longingly of her lost companions, and wondered what they were doing.

Yvonne's life was divided into two well-defined sections. The hours she spent with the other girls, under the supervision of various sisters, were utter misery to the child. Knowing she was in disgrace with the Abbess, the others did not hesitate to treat her with scorn and unkindness; the slightest fault was punished with severity; whippings, bread-and-water diet, solitary hours kneeling on the chapel floor, were often Yvonne's portion. But, when the time came that she was allowed to be with Sister Marie Gabrielle, then Yvonne was happy indeed, whether in the garden gathering herbs, weeding or planting, or in the still-room, lending her little aid in making syrups, ointments, and physics of all sorts.

The herb garden was Yvonne's great delight. Over an acre in extent, it was surrounded by high, massive walls of rough grey stone, in the crevices of which there grew stonecrop, pennywort, gilly-flowers, and many other wee green things. The paths were flagged, and all the beds were edged with neat borders of well-kept box. In one corner grew the violets, and Yvonne would stand with great delight inhaling the fragrant scent which the modest little flowers shed so abundantly on the spring air. She loved to gather both flowers and leaves for Sister Marie Gabrielle, who made, with the juice derived from the flowers mixed with honey, a pleasant syrup for babies' coughs, and, with the leaves, healing plasters and poultices for wounds.

Against a south wall there stood a row of beehives, and Sister Marie Gabrielle told Yvonne many interesting things about the bees: how clever the little insects were, some gathering nectar from the flowers which presently would become honey, and others gathering the pollen. She bade her watch at the entrance to the hive and notice how the bees stood there, fanning their wings and so creating a draught which kept the hives ventilated; and then one day, when the bees swarmed, Sister Marie Gabrielle told Yvonne how the bees were all clustered round their queen, and how they had left the hive in such a large number, leaving only a smaller number to carry on in the old hive while they found a new home.

Yvonne was pleased to hear that, when she was older, she should have a veil and gloves and learn how to manage the busy little creatures herself. Yvonne learnt many things about the herbs that grew so abundantly in that sheltered garden. Sister Marie Gabrielle delighted in talking to the child as the little figure followed her up and down the paths or knelt beside her at work. Sister Marie Gabrielle had, of course, the general mediæval belief in the association of plants with saints, and she told Yvonne that buttercups were St. Anthony's flower; ragwort, St. James's; cowslips, St. Peter's; while St. Barbara, who was Yvonne's patron saint, was specially connected with yellow rocket, and, if she held a little piece in her hand during a thunderstorm, it would ensure safety, for St. Barbara had special control over lightning and would protect those who sought her aid.

Yvonne listened, her big grey eyes fixed on the kindly, wrinkled old face of the nun, then she said slowly: " I ask Jesus to take care of me, sister. The Duchess said—— "

" Hush, hush, my little one ! You had better not talk like that. Remember, the Abbess told you to pray to St. Barbara. I don't want you to get into trouble. Now pick me some of the little green leaves of the yellow rocket. Sister Marie Agathe will welcome them to add to the salad she is making for the Abbess's supper."

If the yellow rocket under discussion failed in protecting those who put their trust in it during thunderstorms, anyhow, it provided a useful addition to the salads.

A large bed in the garden was given over to the growth of betony; it was the special delight of Sister Marie Gabrielle. With it she made oils, ointments, and plaisters.

" Now, remember," she said to Yvonne, " betony is of great value. The good God has made it grow to aid those who cannot digest their meat (food); it also is good for jaundice, gout, and coughs, stitches in the side, and many other things, and when, to-morrow, Mère Baptiste comes with her little baby boy, I shall give her a phial of the liquid for the child's convulsions. If you are a good girl, I will one day ask Sister Marie Tryphosa, who is in charge of the library, to show you a wonderful manuscript which is there. It is beautifully illustrated, and one picture is of a saint discovering the virtue of betony—at least that is what the inscription underneath the picture indicates it to be, although I must say the plant the saint holds in her hand is not much like betony. Now, carry this load to the flagged courtyard and spread it in the sun that it may dry."

The old woman watched the child trot away, and her eyes grew moist and a tender smile played around her lips. Then she sighed.

" Ah me, I fear I am growing too fond of that little one. Did I not renounce all earthly loves when I came here, vowing to love only the Heavenly ? Have I not succeeded in crushing all desire for human love all these years only to find now that little Yvonne is creeping into my heart, and I am loving her with a passion that amazes me. I must make confession of my sin . . . ." She paused. " Ah, dearie me ! If I do, of course my penance will be to be separated from the child. Then she will suffer as well as I. What am I to do ? No, I will not confess. I will hide my weakness even if it means longer in purgatory for my soul. Oh, Mother of God ! " Here the old woman fell on her knees and clasped her hands, wringing them as if in pain. " Mother of God, have pity on a foolish old woman. Have mercy. Lay not this sin to my charge. Plead for me to Thy Holy Child, and forgive my sin."

Long she knelt in that quiet spot, murmuring over and over again: " Mary, have mercy ! " But no peace came to her troubled spirit, no voice responded. The birds trilled their happy songs; the butterflies fluttered over her head; the bees buzzed in joyous harmony; all nature spoke of love and beauty, planned by a loving Father. But the human being, God's highest creation, thought it her duty to seek to crush the power to love planted in her heart by the One above. So dark was her soul, that it seemed to her a sin to cherish the innocent little child in her charge. So twisted, so perverted, can man's ideas become, apart from the teaching of God as given in His Holy Word.

CHAPTER VI

MÈRE BAPTISTE'S BABY

YVONNE liked the days when the peasants and country-folk living in the district came to seek Sister Marie Gabrielle's aid in combating their ailments. As the big heavy doors leading into the outer world slowly swung open, and one after another entered, Yvonne watched with wistful eyes. Outside that door was freedom; somewhere outside was Henri; some day he would come through that door, and she would step out by his side into freedom. Somewhere outside she would find the Duchess and Charlotte. Yvonne never forgot her friends nor Henri's promise; she was only waiting patiently until the day came when Henri, grown up, would be able to fulfil his pledge.

Meanwhile Yvonne was extremely interested in those who entered by that door, and waited in the cloister garth until each one in turn had been treated or advised by Sister Marie Gabrielle. One woman came each week with her delicate baby. Yvonne was attracted by Mère Baptiste, for she had a kind, motherly face, and when one day the wee baby was crying noisily, Sister Marie Gabrielle said to Yvonne, "Take Mère Baptiste to the seat in the garden, Yvonne, the baby disturbs my other patients," Yvonne obeyed with alacrity.

The baby ceased to cry as Mère Baptiste and she seated themselves on the stone seat under the south wall, and Yvonne inquired: " What is his name ? "

" Henri," the mother replied, and Yvonne was delighted.

" I've got a friend called that, and he's coming one day to take me away from here. I have only to wait till he's big enough to do it."

" My little maid, you mustn't say that," the woman replied. " You are going to be a nun. You will be a very holy woman. You must not think of your friend Henri. You had better say a prayer to the blessed Virgin Mary, and ask her to help you to forget him."

Yvonne looked at her gravely, and said: " I pray to God and to my Saviour, Jesus Christ, who died on the Cross for me. I do not pray to the saints or to the Virgin Mary."

" My little maid ! " the woman again exclaimed, this time with horror in her tones. She crossed herself and went on: " Don't the ladies here teach you better than that ? "

" They do try to," Yvonne replied. " But I feel inside here "—she placed her hand on her chest— " that God hears me when I speak to Him, and He makes me happy even when I'm locked in the cell and kept without my dinner. The Duchess told me to pray to God in the name of Jesus Christ."

" Well, well," said Mère Baptiste, " I've got a little maid of my own, and I wouldn't get you into trouble for anything. But, little miss, don't talk like this to the others, and do try to give up such ideas. 'Twill only mean difficulty for you, I fear."

" I can't give it up. It's gone too deep."

Yvonne looked into the motherly face bent over her, and suddenly a longing came into her heart that this woman might know the happiness that she herself had, so she said: " Oh, I wish you loved Jesus, too. Jesus loves you and your little baby. He said when He was here: ' Let the little children come unto Me,' and He took a little child into His arms and blest him one day."

A message then came from Sister Marie Gabrielle to say she was ready to see the sick baby, so Mère Baptiste returned to the building and Yvonne lingered in the garden.

Mère Baptiste shortly returned to her home, but the words Yvonne had spoken remained in her mind. She seemed to hear the little voice saying: " I wish you loved Jesus, too."

" Dear little maid," she said to herself. " I don't know if she is wrong or whether she is on the way to become a saint. But there, poor as I am and hard-working as my little Nanette will have to be, I wouldn't like her to change places with the little lady. Nanette will have her freedom and she has a mother's love, and goodness alone knows what might happen to that poor little maid shut in there, for some of those nuns have hard faces—most of them, in fact, except old Sister Marie Gabrielle."

Presently Nanette came in from the fields, soon to be followed by her father—good, hard-working Jacques. The mother bustled round, while Jacques took the little Henri into his arms and held him tenderly, looking anxiously at the wee white face with the blue veins so clearly showing.

" The little one looks thinner, I fear, Brigette," the father said. " We must light a candle for him and offer a prayer to Saint Joseph, asking for healing for our little son."

The mother placed a steaming bowl of broth on the table, also smaller bowls and wooden spoons, a platter of black bread, and some onions, before she replied. Then she said, " I took him to Saint Anne's Well on my way home from the convent, but I could not find it in my heart to dip him, it seemed so chilly, but I bathed his face with the water. It might perchance do some good."

She served ample portions of the savoury soup and then told them of the little maiden who had talked to her in the convent garden.

Nanette was interested at once.

" Mother ! Is she a little nun ? "

" She will be when she is older. She is only a little maid about your age now, Nanette, but she wears the black robe and the starched cap as the others do who are older. Poor little maid ! She knows not a mother's love as you do, nor can she ever leave that place, shut in like a little caged bird."

" Like our jackdaw that we had in the cage that Father made last year ? " Nanette asked.

" Yes," Nanette's mother replied.

" Oh, I shouldn't like that. I like to run and run in the meadow, and climb the trees and peep into the birds' nests, and wade in the stream."

Nanette's mother and father smiled at their eager little daughter's words. Then Jacques, who was ever slow to speak, said: " What did you say the little nun told you ? "

Brigette repeated Yvonne's words. She said, " I wish you loved Jesus. He loves you and your little baby. I pray to God and to my Saviour, Jesus Christ, who died on the Cross for me."

Jacques crossed himself devoutly and then remarked slowly: " Seems to me, wife, that I've heard that heretics talk like that. We don't know much about them here, living under the shadow of the convent as it were, so, of course, we are all good Roman Catholics; but neighbour Fontaine told me that his sister, who is in service in Paris, says that heretical doctrines are much on the increase, and the priests are taking active steps to suppress such ideas, so we had better beware and hold our tongues on such matters. That little maid will surely be taught better by the good sisters."

So saying, Jacques rose from his seat to return to his labour in the fields. Jacques earned his livelihood by farming a few acres of ground which, with the little farmhouse in which he and his family lived, he rented from the convent authorities. Simple, hard-working folk he and his wife were, honest, and devoted to each other and their children. The house consisted of one big living-room, from the rafters of which hung strings of onions, bunches of herbs, and, when a pig had been killed, sides of bacon. In one corner a rough ladder led to an apartment in the roof, and a door in another corner gave access to a " lean-to " where Mère Baptiste did her · household work. All very simple and primitive, but still a home where love ruled, and husband and wife found happiness in working for one another and the little ones.

But sorrow was drawing near that little home. That very night Brigette woke suddenly after a heavy nap, with a sense of alarm. Her baby boy was lying by her side, and she listened for the sound of his breathing. He was strangely silent, and in a panic she placed her hand on the little form. A shrill cry broke from her lips which roused Jacques.

The little Henri was cold, so cold, icy cold, and Brigette knew what that meant.

Jacques sprang to his feet with an inquiry, and Brigette cried, " A light, oh for a light ! "

Jacques seized the tinder box and, after several strikings of the flint, succeeded in getting a spark, which set fire to a bit of burnt rag, and from that he lighted the home-made rush candle.

Bending anxiously over the child, shielding the light with his toil-worn hand, he gazed into the little wax-like face, so small, so still, so peaceful, just like a little marble image, beautiful even in death—the long dark lashes resting on the wee white cheeks. The tiny lips seemed to be almost smiling; but the father groaned, and the mother asked no question.

Gently Jacques loosened her hold and whispered: " He's gone, our pretty little one, gone ! "

" Gone ! " Brigette echoed the word. " Gone ! But where—where has he gone ? "

Alas ! Jacques could give no answer. Visions of horror, or purgatory, of all they had heard of the terrible uncertainty of the future state of all who had departed from this world filled their minds, and they knew no source of comfort or consolation. All was darkness. Brigette and Jacques mourned without hope, and little Nanette sobbed piteously when morning broke and she was told that her little brother was dead.

CHAPTER VII

" OUT OF THE MOUTH OF BABES "

" MOTHER, you did say you would take me to see the little nun-lady one day," Nanette reminded her mother of her promise.

Brigette Baptiste sighed. The mention of Yvonne brought to her memory the scene in the convent garden, the eager little face of the child-novice as she looked at baby Henri, and then spoke of the love of Christ for children. And now baby Henri was buried beneath the churchyard sod and his soul . . . His mother shivered.

" Mother of God, gracious Lady, have mercy upon the soul of my little white dove," she prayed.

" Mother ! "

Nanette waited for a reply.

" Yes, child, I ought to go to the convent. The good sister will be wondering how her little patient is, unless she has heard of his death. Father Benedict, who buried him, may have thought to tell the sister. It seems to me that although the Lady Abbess and the sisters are shut behind high walls and strongly barred doors, yet they hear a good deal of what happens in the outside world."

" Sister Marie Agathe and Sister Marie Mathilde are often in the village, Mother. If they come out, why may not the little nun-lady who talked to you ? Could she not come and run in the fields with me?"

"Nay, nay, child. She is to take her vows as soon as she is old enough; she must be kept unspotted from the world. Sister Marie Agathe and Sister Marie Mathilde are lay-sisters."

"What are lay-sisters, Mother?"

"As far as I can make out, Nanette, they are under promise of obedience to the convent authorities, and may never marry; but they have not taken the vows the others have, so they may come out. They are there to serve the ladies."

"And, Mother, what is the world? Is it the fields and the trees, the birds and the brook?"

"Ah, my little Nanette, now you've asked me something. Ah, indeed, what is the world?"

"Well," said Nanette musingly, "perhaps the little nun-lady would get spotted if she ran about with me. I know my frock does, but I should think she could get spotted in the convent garden and kitchens just as much as outside."

"Ah, my little pigeon, you think too much. But we will go and see the good Sister Marie Gabrielle soon, and maybe you will have sight of the young lady."

So Brigette Baptiste took Nanette to the convent, and, while she talked to Sister Marie Gabrielle and told the sad story of her little Henri, Sister Marie Gabrielle called Yvonne, and said, "Take the little girl to the garden and show her where the birds take their bath; and see if you can find the tortoise, but don't go too near to the hives."

At first the children were rather shy. Yvonne

looked with great admiration at Nanette. She wore no bonnet or cap, and the sunbeams seemed to have got entangled in her curly hair which hung loosely round her neck and shoulders. Her dark eyes sometimes looked like the velvet petals of a pansy, and yet again like the smoke that rose in a spiral thread from the woodman's fire of chips. Her limbs were shapely and brown from exposure to sun and air. Altogether the child of the peasant farmer was a sight to please more critical eyes than those of little Yvonne.

Nanette for her part regarded the little lady who looked like a miniature nun with great awe, but soon in the interest and charm of the garden they forgot to be shy and chattered happily.

At one end of the garden was the tool-house, and there on a bed of hay lay Grimalkin, the big, grey tabby-cat, with four wee kittens, and both children laughed merrily as they watched the little animals.

Presently Nanette said, " My little brother is dead."

" Oh-h. I wondered why your mother had not brought him."

Nanette's little face clouded.

" I wish he hadn't died. I did ask St. Anne to heal him, and mother took him to St. Anne's Well and put some of the water on his forehead, but he died all the same. I wonder where he is now."

" Oh, don't you know ? " Yvonne exclaimed. " Jesus took him, and Heaven is such a happy place. The Duchess told me about it."

" Oh, do tell me," Nanette said eagerly.

Together the little maidens sat down on the step of the tool-house door, and Yvonne, delighted to have such a willing listener, talked enthusiastically.

"It's a place where no one ever cries, and no one is ever unkind, and no one has any pain. Everybody is happy and loving and no one is ever naughty, not the teeniest little bit, and the loveliest bit of all is that Jesus is there."

Yvonne paused for breath, but Nanette was listening, so she continued. "And one thing I'm so glad about it is, it is never dark there. I don't like the dark. Sister Marie Thérèse sends me into the dark cells and into the dormitory 'cause, she says, I'm a little coward, and the dark creeps all round one so, but it's never going to be dark in Heaven."

"If no one is ever naughty there, I don't believe I'll be able to go there, I'm ever so naughty, lots of times."

A little flash of merriment showed in those gridelin eyes. Nanette rather enjoyed her reputation for naughtiness.

"So am I," said Yvonne, but her tone was sad.

"Oh, are you? What do you do that's naughty? Tell me—do you steal the apples?"

"No, no," Yvonne replied in horror. What would happen to her if ever she were guilty of such a misdeed! "No, it's naughty inside that I am. When Sister Marie Thérèse whips me I want to kill her, I feel so angry; and one day when one of the girls kept on calling me a heretic, I bit her."

Nanette's eyes danced. She was thrilled at the

account of Yvonne's behaviour.

"What happened to you then?" she asked.

"I was whipped, and I had to lie on the refectory floor all the time the others were having dinner, and when they left the refectory one of them stepped on me."

"Oh-h, I should have screamed if they had done that to me."

"It wouldn't be any good. But don't let us talk about it."

"Well, anyhow, you won't be able to go to Heaven; you'll be outside with me," said Nanette cheerfully.

"Oh no, no. I shall be able to go, and you mustn't be outside, Nanette."

"But how?" queried Nanette. "You're naughty, and you said naughty people aren't there."

"I'll tell you all about it. The Duchess told me. I am a sinner, but the Lord Jesus knew all about it, and He said, ' I'll bear the punishment for Yvonne's sins, and if she is sorry for her sin, she can be forgiven and go toHeaven '; and I am sorry. I feel a big ache inside me when I think about them, and it makes me cry to think Jesus had to bear such a big punishment for me; and I tell Him so, and He forgives me and comforts me, and I shall go to Heaven because Jesus died, and that's the reason your little baby has gone there too."

"I am glad. I'll tell mother not to cry any more. Is baby very happy in Heaven?"

"Yes. He isn't ill any more, 'cause there's no more pain there."

"My mother will be glad to know that. But tell me, what punishment did the Lord Jesus bear for your sins?"

So Yvonne told her, seated there in that convent garden, where many a nun with burdened heart had worked and walked; where never before had the sweet story of forgiveness and love been told in simple, childlike language; the completeness of the Saviour's sacrifice to make atonement for sin needing no additional work, no penance, no deed of merit on the part of man. Clearly little Yvonne told, and Nanette listened breathlessly. She gave a little cry of dismay when Yvonne spoke of the soldier's sword that pierced the Saviour's side; she smiled and clapped her hands with glee as she heard how He rose from the grave; and when Yvonne paused, she said, " I wish He'd done all that for me."

" It was for you, and He loves you, Nanette."

" And is He really alive to-day?"

" Yes, oh yes. I know He is, because I often feel that He is with me."

" Then He isn't like the big crucifix in the church, and the one in the shrine by the roadside. I thought we prayed to the saints because Jesus was dead and couldn't hear us. I am so glad. I'll tell mother and father all about it."

Then, with a sudden swift change of thought so characteristic of a child, she said, " Do let us see the kitties again," and a few moments afterwards both children were laughing merrily and cuddling the kittens as if they had never had a serious thought in their lives.

The children were quite unaware that there

had been a listener to their conversation. Some little time before, Sister Marie Gabrielle had come into the garden to fetch Nanette. Her movements were always quiet, and she had drawn near to the side of the tool-house, and had paused to listen to their voices, high-pitched and clear; their childish speech carried easily, and each word was distinct.

Sister Marie Gabrielle sighed, and a tear rolled down her cheek. Could it be possibly true that the death of Christ on the Cross was sufficient to put away sin? Oh, that burden of sin! How it pressed on her heart. For years she had toiled unremittingly, hoping by her prayers, her fastings, her long night vigils in the convent chapel, to lessen the load. Ever present in her mind was the thought: "Am I doing enough? Am I accumulating merit? Am I shortening those awful years in purgatory which lie beyond this world?"

Years, many years ago, when Sister Marie Gabrielle was in the world, she, the beautiful young Estelle de St. Legier was loved and sought by a worthy suitor. Home, marriage, wifehood, motherhood, these the prospect before her, all alluring. But the sense of sin had even then been so great that the thought of it haunted her. "What will all this profit me if I lose my soul? I must make my salvation." So, voluntarily, although it scarred wounds in her young heart, she turned away from all earthly enticements, and took the veil with the one only ambition, to save her soul; and now, in her seventy-fifth year, she felt herself no nearer attainment, still as far from her goal as ever.

Was Yvonne right? Was the Saviour's death sufficient without any aid from her? If only she could believe that, what untold rest it would bring to her burdened heart. How real Christ seemed to little Yvonne, she thought, and then said to herself, " I honour the Christ, the Son of the blessed Virgin, too."

She started, for a voice sounded in her soul, and so vivid was it that she thought for the moment someone spoke. " What is your Christ? A helpless Babe in His Mother's arms; a dead Man on a crucifix; a wafer held aloft in the priest's hand for your worship? Nay, I am He that liveth."

But then came the thought, had all her sacrifice been in vain? Did all her good deeds go for nothing? Ah, it was not easy to give up faith in her own meritorious actions. Surely they counted for something. On saints' days no drop of water or crumb of bread ever passed her lips. How many hours of the night, when others slept, did she spend in the constant repetition of prayers? How often she lay prostrate before the life-size image of the crucified Christ in the chapel! Besides which, never had she turned aside from the most loathsome task, often welcoming the opportunity of attending to unspeakably horrible wounds, that she might add to her merit and atone for at least some of her sins.

" Ah me," she thought, " I am too old to change my ideas," and with another sigh she came into sight and told Yvonne to take Nanette to her mother.

E

CHAPTER VIII

IMPRISONED

CHARLOTTE DE BOURBON knelt by her mother's side in that lady's boudoir. The child's face was pale and her lips trembled, but no tears fell. Charlotte had just remarked to her mother, " I have cried and cried till I haven't a tear left to shed."

The Duchess, too, was outwardly calm, although her heart was wrung with anguish.

Charlotte had passed her thirteenth birthday, and the Duke had said that the time had come when she must enter the convent of Jouarre. Both Charlotte and her mother knew that they were powerless to alter that decree. Charlotte had flung herself at her father's feet, she had sobbed, begged, protested, but all in vain. Bigotry, self-will, ambition, and, above all, a petty desire to thwart his wife had overcome any slight fatherly feeling he had for his daughter. His word was law, no one had ever opposed his will, and, supported by ecclesiastical authority, the Duke de Montpensier determined to carry out his project. He was annoyed, seriously annoyed, at the opposition of his wife and daughter.

"What fools women are," he said to his confessor. " Cannot they understand that Charlotte will hold a higher position as the Abbess of Jouarre—which I intend she shall be as soon

as she is old enough, and the old Abbess dies—
than anything this world could offer her ? "

So Charlotte had come to the last day at
home. To-morrow she must go with her father
to the convent; to-morrow she must say " good-
bye " to the old château, the gardens, the horses
in the stable, the dogs in the kennels, all of whom
she reckoned as her friends. Within a few days
her pretty silken frocks must be laid aside, her
long, abundant hair cut off, the coarse, woollen
frock and starched cap donned, and she must
resign herself to a life of imprisonment.

" Oh, Mother, Mother," she wailed. " I don't
want religion; I don't want prayers and services
and fastings and penances; I want parties; I
want to ride my pony over the fields; I want to
marry; I want little children of my own; I
want—— "

" Hush, hush, my child. I want you to listen
very carefully to what I am going to tell you. I
have spent long hours in prayer for you ever
since your father told me of his wish three years
ago, and I have the conviction that somehow,
sometime, God is going to deliver you from that
life of bondage into which you are going to be
forced. I believe God means you to serve Him
as a happy wife and mother, and, in order to help
you to leave the convent when God shall open
the door for you, I have prepared a document
setting out your views, and how it is absolutely
against your wish and mine that you enter the
convent; consequently, any vows that you are
compelled to make will not be binding. I wish
you to sign this paper, Charlotte my child, and

remember what I say—that you are free to leave your cloistered life when the opportunity comes, as it will do. Meanwhile, dear heart, seek to be patient and contented, do not rebel against your life. Oh, my Charlotte, how I wish that I felt sure that you know the Lord Jesus as your own Saviour. I have sought to teach you of Him, whom to know is life eternal."

" Mother, I promise you I will try. I will never forget what you have taught me."

The Duchess produced the document she had prepared, and Charlotte signed it. Then together they knelt in prayer, and the Duchess commended her child to the keeping of God. Rising from their knees, the Duchess placed her hands on her daughter's head and said, " The Lord bless thee and keep thee; the Lord make His face to shine upon thee and give thee peace."

" Mother ! Mother ! Mother ! " was all Charlotte could say.

The Duchess could hardly speak. Her heart was wrung with anguish, but she spoke quietly, " Now, my child, you must go to your rest. Your father wishes to make an early start in the morning."

Charlotte, almost as tall as her mother, flung her arms round her parent in one long, sorrowful embrace, and then with a choking sob she turned and went to her room.

Next morning both were calm, and the Duke congratulated himself that there was no scene as he had anticipated. With Charlotte it was the calmness of despair, with her mother the calmness of trust in God."

The Duke was gruff.

" Come, come," he said, " say your farewells. It is but *au revoir.* Your mother will be coming to see you, Charlotte, after a few months have elapsed."

But the Duke was mistaken. Never again in this world was the Duchess to see the winsome face of her dearly loved daughter. Never again was Charlotte to fling her young strong arms around her mother in close embrace. Nothing was left for Charlotte but a memory: a memory of love and patience, a memory that was to colour all her thoughts and desires as long as she should live.

When the Duke on his stately charger rode up to the convent gate, followed by his band of men all well mounted, surrounding Charlotte on her loved chestnut horse, there was great commotion: the massive doors were flung open; the lay-sister in charge sent her assistant to hastily notify the Abbess of the arrival. That lady came speedily, and with due ceremony received her noble visitor.

The Abbess knew full well that Louis de Bourbon, the Duke de Montpensier, had power at Court, that ecclesiastical dignitaries of the Church of Rome listened to his opinions, and she felt flattered that he had decided to entrust his daughter to her care. So Charlotte's reception was vastly different to that accorded to Yvonne some years before, but it by no means mitigated Charlotte's sorrow, as the big doors closed behind her father, as before long he took his departure, and with the feeling of a helpless captive she followed the Abbess, who herself condescended to show Mademoiselle de Bourbon the cell she was to occupy.

Just then Yvonne was in the sick-room with a heavy cold, and so was unaware of Charlotte's arrival. Next day at the recreation hour, when all the young novices were walking in the garden, with the exception of Charlotte, who was receiving her preliminary instructions in the Abbess's room, many of the girls were discussing the new arrival. Some of them had caught a glimpse of the splendour of the cavalcade which had accompanied Charlotte to the convent, for the Duke had taken pains that the Abbess and other inmates should be impressed by his daughter's importance, and had arrived with a considerable retinue; now more than one of the young people expressed the determination that Charlotte should be her own particular friend.

Yvonne, who had been allowed out for an airing for a short time as her cold was better, remembering how young she had been on her arrival, experienced a faint hope that this new-comer might be a small child. " If she is," she thought, " I'll try to take care of her."

Presently she ventured to ask, " How old is she ? "

Some of the girls at once said, " She won't be your friend, Yvonne," one adding, " Her father is a good Catholic, and she won't be tainted with heretical doctrines, as we all know you are; she'll be horrified at you." There was quite a chorus of voices saying, " She won't have anything to do with you."

Yvonne shrank away in silence. Although a child who naturally had plenty to say, she had learnt in the hard school of experiences to refrain from replying to the taunts of these older girls. She felt sad as she thought: " No one will ever want to be friendly with me."

Not many minutes afterwards, Charlotte, released from the Abbess's tuition, came sauntering down the grass path between the rose bushes. A little silence fell upon the group of girls. They felt a trifle shy, and Charlotte glanced from one to the other, coolly critical. She was wondering if among these girls she would find anyone companionable. Then her eye fell on the quiet little face of Yvonne, as she stood a little apart from the others, and Charlotte looked at her with a puzzled air. Then, with a rush, she bounded forward calling excitedly, " Yvonne, Yvonne, is it really you ? "

Yvonne looked bewildered for a moment, then, although over three years had passed since the children had been separated, and both had grown considerably, memory revived, and Yvonne turned to her friend's outstretched arms and, regardless of the amazement of the others, they hugged each other and laughed with joy."

" No one told me you were here," Charlotte said, and Yvonne replied simply, " I expect they had forgotten all about me."

The others had recovered speech and now crowded round asking questions.

Charlotte kept her arm round Yvonne and answered to their enquiries: " Yvonne was my very dearest friend years ago, before she came here, and she will be my friend now."

"But," objected one, "she is in disgrace with the Abbess. She is really a heretic."

"Heretic!" Charlotte replied with scorn. "I don't care anything about that. I'll be one too, if Yvonne wants me to be, very likely."

At that time Charlotte's religious principles were not deeply rooted; conviction of the need of salvation was yet to come.

"Come on, Yvonne," she continued, calmly ignoring the others; "take me to some quiet spot where we can talk. We've heaps to tell each other."

So Yvonne led the way to the herb garden, while the girls, disappointed at the turn of affairs, remained behind to discuss the situation with much heat.

CHAPTER IX

CALLED HOME

THE days passed slowly with much monotony for Charlotte. The presence of Yvonne somewhat lessened her dislike to her new life, but she sorely missed the freedom she had enjoyed in her father's château surrounded by its wide acres of park-land and gardens. She never grew tired of talking to Yvonne about her horse, her dogs, the fishing in the meadow stream; and Yvonne was a sympathetic listener. One day Charlotte told her friend in subdued whispers of the Duchess's conviction that some day she would be set free from her prison and of the paper she had signed.

Yvonne exclaimed: " Oh, Charlotte, when Henri comes for me, you will be able to come too; we'll go together."

Charlotte, being older, realised some of the difficulties which had not occurred to Yvonne, and she said, " I don't know what to think, Yvonne. Father will never, never let me come home, and where should I go ? "

" But we'll be grown-up then, Charlotte."

" Well, it doesn't seem to me that grown-up people can do what they like, any more than children. I know mother can't. I know she would have been to see me before this, but I can just hear father saying, ' Certainly not, Jaqueline, you will only unsettle the child ! ' "

"But she will come some day, won't she?
Oh, I do hope the Abbess will let me see her
when she comes. I do love her so."

And so they talked. Poor children!

Months passed, and then one day a messenger
wearing the livery of the Duke de Montpensier
arrived at the convent and sought speech with
the Lady Abbess.

After his departure the Abbess sent for Sister
Marie Thérèse, who was in charge of the novices,
to tell her of the tidings the Duke's messenger
had brought.

Sister Marie Thérèse kissed the hem of the
Abbess's robe, and stood with downcast eyes
and meekly folded hands.

The Abbess spoke abruptly as was her wont.

"The Duchess de Montpensier is dying."

"Indeed," replied Sister Marie Thérèse.

"The Duke wishes us to prepare Charlotte for
bad tidings, for the end is not far off. He does
not wish Charlotte to go to her mother, although
I gather from the messenger that the Duchess
implores that she should see her child once
again; but the Duke is wise, he says he trusts
Charlotte is reconciled to her life here, and that
under our influence she is becoming ardent in her
religious exercises. To come home would probably hinder the good work which he fondly hopes
has begun in her."

Sister Marie Thérèse's eyes flashed. She saw
more of Charlotte than the Abbess did, and she
had her doubts, but she kept silent and waited
for the Abbess to continue.

"I will see Charlotte and tell her of her

mother's serious illness, but I shall not tell her that her father forbids her leaving the convent to visit her mother—not, at any rate, at first. I wish her to believe that it is entirely my decision. It gives me an opportunity to give Charlotte a taste of my power. Although she is outwardly submissive, I always feel there is a veiled insolence about the girl, and I intend to take this chance of subduing her."

Sister Marie Thérèse murmured, " In this you show your wisdom."

" You may fetch her," the Abbess said shortly, and, while Sister Marie Thérèse went, she sat musing.

The Abbess had long known that the Duke meant Charlotte to be her successor, and the presence of the girl in the convent was a constant reminder to the aged woman that life was slipping away. It was distasteful indeed to her to think of Charlotte with her buoyant youth, her quick, active brain, and her attractive personality, reigning as Abbess when she herself would be forgotten, or, at best, remembered with a sense of relief that her power was over, for the Abbess knew she was not popular. She ruled by fear, not by love. To possess power had always been a ruling ambition with her, and obtaining it in her little kingdom had had a baneful effect, which is the usual consequence when one human being possesses complete control over others, especially if that one happens to be of a petty disposition.

Charlotte followed Sister Marie Thérèse into the room with wonder. As she made the customary salutation she was rapidly recalling some of her mischievous deeds during the last few days, and trying to decide for which she was going to be called to give an account. But there was little time for thought.

The Abbess said: "Charlotte, I have had tidings from your home to-day. Your father sends to say that your mother is ill—— "

Charlotte interrupted. "Then I must go home at once."

The Abbess frowned heavily. Not an inmate of that building, not even Sister Marie Gabrielle, dared to break in on her speech in that way.

She continued coldly. "That I shall not permit, Charlotte. You can repair to the chapel and spend two hours before the crucifix, repeating a suitable prayer for your mother's soul. Take your rosary with you and count your prayers, and report to me how many times you repeat the words. Sister Marie Thérèse shall select the prayer for you."

Charlotte looked stunned for a moment, but she quickly recovered, and exclaimed: "But I must go to my mother. I am sure she would wish it. I need not stay long, but I must go."

"Charlotte, I do not intend that you shall go. You are completely under my control. You must learn that a nun should have no will of her own. Absolute obedience is necessary for a holy life, and you must practise it. We shall probably hear in the morning that your mother is dead, then I shall give orders that all are to recite a prayer for her soul. Now go."

Charlotte stood her ground and spoke impressively.

"Reverend Mother, you do not understand. I love my mother, and I only ask to be allowed to return home with my father's messenger. I promise to come back in a few days. I am not a nun yet, and I have never promised obedience to you. Please, please let me go."

The Abbess was growing seriously angry. Charlotte looked so determined; she was not her father's daughter for nothing, and she was now nearly fifteen, tall, and well developed for her age. But the Abbess only took a greater interest in breaking Charlotte's will; here was a character worth crushing. So she rose from her chair and said, "Charlotte, go at once and spend two hours as I have directed. After that I shall have to deal with you for your insolence in daring to question my command."

Then Charlotte's self-control gave way. She flung herself on the floor, and shriek after shriek rent the air.

The two women stood looking at her, then the Abbess said, "Call Sister Marie Agathe, and carry her to her cell. Make her understand that she can scream as long as she chooses, no one will take any heed. Lock her in and bring me the key."

The Abbess's word was obeyed, and poor Charlotte sobbed herself into a state of utter exhaustion.

Within a few days tidings came that the Duchess had passed away. Charlotte received the news in silence, and the Abbess congratulated herself that she had subdued the girl's turbulent spirit. But Charlotte was by no means subdued, only her common sense showed her it was futile to match her strength of will and purpose against that of the Abbess. She was too proud to plead, of too high a courage to cringe. With calm dignity she accepted the severe penance prescribed for her, and held herself aloof from all. The result of the experience she had passed through was to change her from a high-spirited girl to a woman with a touch of grimness in her disposition which manifested itself to all, save Yvonne; with her, Charlotte was tenderness itself. Charlotte suffered much in those days, and she had not yet learnt the sympathy and love of Christ. That the Saviour cared for and could comfort anyone was only an idea, a theory held by her mother and Yvonne. So her heart ached, and more and more she felt a distaste for convent life; yet she did not seek and find consolation as she might have done, at the feet of the Saviour.

It was some days before Yvonne had any opportunity of converse with Charlotte, for Charlotte was not allowed to mix with the others while her punishment lasted. But when she was permitted to return to the ordinary course of life, Yvonne's tears mingled with her friend's, and together they mourned the loss of the Duchess.

" But, Charlotte," Yvonne said one day, " we must not forget that she is happy. She loved Jesus, and she is with Him now."

" I hope so, Yvonne, but how can we know ? The Reverend Mother says, ' Pray for your mother's soul that it may be released from purgatory,' and I heard Sister Marie Thérèse say to Sister Marie Agathe, ' The Duchess was a Protestant, why waste our prayers on her ? ' "

" But, Charlotte, we know what the Duchess taught us: that if we trust Jesus, if we know that He died on the Cross to atone for our sins, we shall go straight to Him when we die."

" Dear heart, I'm not good like you. You seem to remember all mother taught you, and I feel so muddled. Father said one thing and the Reverend Mother says the same as he did; and you talk so differently, and so did mother. I get confused. How do you remember so well ? "

" I think I can tell. The last day I was with the Duchess she said, ' Little Yvonne, ask God to give you His Holy Spirit in your heart, and the Holy Spirit will be your teacher. He will keep you from forgetting.' And I did ask, and the Holy Spirit does teach me. It all seems more real to me every day, and when I can talk to you or to Mère Baptiste or Nanette—I can't explain exactly—it seems as though Jesus was quite close, telling me what to say."

" Do Mère Baptiste and Nanette like to hear ? "

" Yes, indeed they do, Charlotte. I believe they both love Jesus. You do love Him, too, don't you, dearest ? "

" I don't know. I think I do a bit. But I asked Him not to let me come here, and I was so disappointed."

" Never mind, dear heart. Some day God is going to open the door and let us go free. I feel sure of it somehow."

CHAPTER X

HENRI'S BETROTHAL

M. DE VALOIS, Henri's father, sat in meditation. Presently he rang a bell which stood on a table beside him, and to the page who answered his summons he gave directions to fetch his son, as he desired his presence.

The room in which M. de Valois sat was panelled in dark oak and furnished in sombre fashion. A desk of heavy black wood stood in the window, upon which was a metal inkpot, a sand dish, and an hour-glass. The windows were of coloured glass through which the daylight filtered hazily, giving to Henri, as he entered from the brilliant light of the garden, a feeling of impending disaster, but he assured himself that it was only the effect of the gloomy interior after the freshness of the open air.

Henri was now a tall, handsome lad of fifteen years, dressed in a suit of green cloth buttoned high at the neck. He knelt on entering and respectfully saluted his parent, who smiled and said, " Be seated, my son, for I have much to say to you, and I would have you give me your careful attention."

M. de Valois smiled genially, and there was a look of pride and satisfaction in his eyes as he gazed at his boy. As Henri took a low stool, his father said with a note of pleasantry in his voice, " I hope what I have to tell you, Henri, will give you pleasure. You have come to an age when I consider it advisable that you should be betrothed. You are all I possess now, my lad, and I am anxious to do the very best for you, so I have entered into contract with M. de St. Barbe, and we have decided that you are to be betrothed without delay to his daughter Rénée. She is fourteen years old, and, her father assures me, is of an amiable disposition, has been well governed, and will make you an excellent wife. She will bring with her a considerable dowry, and, most important of all, she comes from a staunch Roman Catholic family, and nowadays, when so many of our best families are tainted with heresy, I congratulate myself that I have secured a bride for you of our own religion, as well as being wealthy and charming. What do you say to your good fortune, my boy? "

Henri seemed speechless, and his father added, " Of course, you understand that although the betrothal ceremony will take place shortly, a few years must elapse before Rénée becomes your bride. Say, three years; meanwhile your training as a soldier will occupy that period of time."

He paused, and waited for his son to speak.

" Well? " he said interrogatively.

" Father, I do not wish to marry Rénée de St. Barbe. I have other plans."

Henri's father smiled indulgently.

" You are maturing early, Henri; but let me hear what these plans are."

" I crave your pardon, sir; but, long ago, I determined that if ever I married, Yvonne

F

d'Arande would be my bride." Henri flushed.

M. de Valois' brow puckered in perplexity.
" Yvonne d'Arande," he repeated, then memory
revived. " Oh, that child ! But, Henri, are you
forgetting that Yvonne is dedicated to Holy
Mother Church ? She is a *religieuse*; it is impossible for her to live a secular life."

" Dedicated you say, sir, but by whom ? It
was against her will that she entered the convent.
Will God be pleased with an unwilling sacrifice ?
Vows forced upon her by the decree of others
will not be binding."

M. de Valois was surprised at his son's reason-
ing powers, but he chose to treat the argument
lightly.

" Tut, tut, lad ! She was but an infant when
you saw her last. By now she is probably
reconciled to her life, charmed with the delights
of religion. Besides, it would be impossible for
her to leave the convent or for you to have speech
with her. No, no, you must put all such ideas from
you, and accept my planning for you. I have
had more experience of the world than you have
had, and I know what is best for your future."

"But, Father, it may not be as impossible as
you think for Yvonne to leave the convent. Have
you not heard of Katherine von Bora, and how
she with eight others left a convent in Nimptsch,
and how afterwards she became the wife of
Martin Luther ? "

Again Henri's father gasped with amazement
at his son's knowldege, and he asked, " How do
you know this ? "

" My tutor told me the story, because he knows

that I intend to rescue Yvonne some day."

"Nonsense, lad! Anyone hearing you talk would think you were a Protestant, but you argue in vain. I called you hither to tell you of the arrangements made for your future, not to listen to such wild suggestions as you are making."

M. de Valois paused, and Henri, with a crimson flush flooding his face, said quietly: "Father, I am a Protestant."

"Henri! I have always thought you a sensible lad with well-developed brain, but I shall begin to think you are taking leave of your senses. What do you know of Protestant principles?"

"Father, the Duchess de Montpensier, before she died, taught me the truth. She studied God's Word, and I believe—— "

Henri's father was growing impatient. He was an indulgent father for those days, and had always allowed Henri freedom of speech, a thing few fathers permitted, but now his patience was almost exhausted. He was about to speak imperiously, when his eye fell on a painting on the wall—an almost life-size portrait of a beautiful girl with a face full of sunshine, lips just parted as if she were about to speak. Tears dimmed M. de Valois' eyes. He felt as though his sweet young English wife was saying again what she had said on her death-bed some six years previously, "Be gentle with our boy, dearest."

So instead of the stern words which he had almost uttered he said, "Henri, my boy, do not disappoint me. You are all I have; your mother and little sister have been taken from me, and if you insist on being a Protestant it would be an insurmountable barrier between us. Remember you are a Roman Catholic, as I am, and as for any further thought of that child Yvonne, it is madness."

Henri knew it was useless to say anything more, and he listened in silence to all his father told of the prospect which lay before him; he longed to protest, he was dismayed at the net spread for his feet, but yet his father's pathetic appeal touched him deeply. He left the room with the words " you are all I have " ringing in his ears, but as he walked about the grounds of the home he loved so dearly he seemed to hear the Duchess saying, as she had some time before, " You have to choose, Henri; Christ or the world; Christ or friends; Christ or home. Which will it be ? "

Henri lifted a pale but resolute face to the evening sky and whispered: " Christ for me."

Presently he sought his old nurse Denise, to whom he poured out his story. She was full of sympathy, but could only tell him that he must yield to his father's will. There seemed no way of escape, and when the time came for the betrothal ceremony it was a sad-faced boy that did the bidding of his elders.

Little Rénée de St. Barbe was extremely excited at her share in the proceedings. She loved being in the limelight, and she took a keen delight in the elegance of her attire for the occasion. She wore a gown of rose-coloured velvet, with an overskirt of silver tissue; round her throat was a fine lace ruff edged with pearls; her cap, too, was of silver tissue; her sleeves were of cream satin; and a magnificent string of rubies was twisted round her neck and then hung over her breast; while the train which swept behind the little figure was of palest pink satin. From beneath her gown her little silver shoes, ornamented with pink roses, peeped out.

Of the other principal actor in the scene Rénée took little notice. Of course there must be a boy, she knew, for a betrothal ceremony, but she was childish for her years and was chiefly concerned with her pretty clothes, the attention of the grown-ups, and, last but by no means least, the feast that was to follow.

Henri, pale and grave, looked almost a man in his suit of cloth of gold, with a short cloak of green velvet lined with cream satin. His high double ruff of gold lace annoyed him, and he disliked the massive gold chain which was twisted round his neck. On his arm he wore his lady's favour which Rénée had, by her mother's directions, pinned on his sleeve; but he congratulated himself that within a week he would have started his training as a soldier and would no longer be bothered with such senseless garments. But, boy-like, when the ceremony was over he forgot for a while his perplexities and reluctance and enjoyed the feast.

The great hall was draped with marvellous tapestries. The gold and silver plate, dishes of finest porcelain, lace napkins, glasses tinted with dainty hues, all made a background for the gorgeously apparelled ladies and gentlemen who filled the hall. The food was of the richest description: boars' heads, caprons stuffed with truffles, whole peacocks, sweetmeats of various kinds, the chief being a wonderful piece of confectionery, a castle moulded out of sugar, each pinnacle and column exquisitely modelled; the structure was hollow, and through the fretted window casements tiny figures could be seen, supposed to represent the principle actors in the day's proceedings. Luscious fruits were piled high on massive silver dishes, and Henri gave himself up with boyish zest to the enjoyment of the many dishes.

But when home again in his father's chateâu, he thought much of his vow and wondered how he should fulfil it. In spite of his father's dictum that he was a Roman Catholic, Henri knew that the teaching he had received from the Duchess had entered too deeply into his heart to permit of his accepting his father's religious views. Simply and sincerely he as a little boy had taken heed to the Gospel story; clearly there stood out in his memory a day when the Duchess had spoken to him of the crucifixoin of the Lord Jesus. Even yet he could hear her gentle voice saying: " Henri, remember when the Saviour gave His life on the cruel cross it was to put away sin, your sin and mine, and no good deeds that you or I could do, no fastings, no penances could add one tiny bit to that complete, full sacrifice which He made. Forgiveness, eternal life, are God's free gifts to us, and we can never merit them; but we can accept them, and, having accepted them, then we can work for the Master, not to win our salvation, but because we love Him."

The Holy Spirit had been working in Henri's heart, child as he was, giving to him a consciousness of sin, and when the Duchess asked: " Henri, are you a sinner ? " he fixed his eyes thoughtfully on her as he answered: " Yes, I know I am."

" Then," continued the Duchess, " Jesus wants to save you, to forgive you, to make you His own. Shall we pray to Him now and ask Him to do this ? "

Henri nodded a mute assent, and together they knelt. The Duchess prayed, and Henri, ten-year-old Henri, whispered his request, and He who welcomed the children when He was here upon earth that day received Henri, setting His seal upon him for evermore.

Henri was much impressed by the Duchess's prayer. There was no crucifix, no Madonna group, no appeal to a saint; simply, with direct, clear language that a child could understand, the Duchess spoke to the Father in the name and for the sake of Jesus Christ. In the years that followed, when Henri was present in the chapel attached to his father's château or in church or cathedral, the air redolent with incense, the life-size figure of the Christ on the Cross, the saints in their niches, the Madonna with her infant Son, the shrine that held the Eucharist, the tiny doors of which gleamed with precious stones—all these he would ignore, and with eyes closed, oblivious of the chanting of the prayers, the constant repetitions and invocations of the saints, he would seek God for himself. Now in his perplexity he prayed, asking God his Father to undertake for him and to make a way in which he should be able to rescue Yvonne, and keep him from denying the Faith.

He grew thoughtful and manly in those days as he listened frequently to the discussions carried on by his father, visitors to the château, and dignitaries of the Romish Church who often found their way to his father's home.

Religious dissension was rife in the land. The Huguenots—adherents of the Reformation—were steadily increasing, but the Queen-Mother, Catharine de Medici, was exerting her influence over her son Charles IX, seeking to organise a great persecution, intending that no Protestant should be left in the land. In vain had the Chancellor de l'Hospital, in a speech on the opening of the first Assembly of the States of the new king's reign, exhorted to religious toleration. That was a virtue to which Catharine was a complete stranger.

The Huguenots were not unaware of the peril of their position and, quietly but none the less determinedly, they were making their plans, for it seemed not unlikely that they might be forced to take up arms in self-defence against the Roman Catholics. Under the leadership of Admiral Coligny, a prince of the royal blood of France and a man of great military talent, the Huguenots were minded not to be caught unprepared.

Henri heard many discussions and listened gravely and silently as his elders spoke of the part he might play as a young soldier. It was taken for granted that should a religious war arise Henri would be on the side of the Catholics, but Henri knew that as soon as he was old enough, whatever it might cost, his decision would be declared and he would throw in his lot with the Huguenots, and if necessary fight on their side.

One thing he was thankful for, that his father had decided on a soldier's career for him, and had not thought of dedicating him to the Church.

CHAPTER XI

THOSE LITTLE HANDS

CHARLOTTE yawned wearily. The task on which she was engaged bored her intensely, although she knew it was considered high honour that she was entrusted with so important a piece of work: the embroidering of a new altar cloth, worked in gold thread, soft silks, and, most tedious of all, hair—fine strands of hair, brown, gold, or auburn; hair cut from the head of many a young maiden on entering the convent. The design was intricate, the stitches varied and numerous, and Charlotte progressed slowly. She began to wish she had pretended to be a bungler at such work, instead of letting it be known that she was skilled in such labour. She envied Yvonne at her work in the garden or helping to care for the sick; or could she have changed places with Sister Marie Tryphosa, who was in charge of the library, it would have pleased Charlotte. She was interested in that wonderful collection of books wherein the wisdom of sages or the folly of mediæval superstitions had been inscribed on vellum or parchment, illuminated with gorgeous colourings and quaint illustrations. It was no consolation to Charlotte to know hers was considered the higher task; she would gladly have exchanged the needle for the spade or duster—activity suited her best.

Just at the moment of the weary yawn Sister

Marie Gabrielle entered the room, and her shrewd, kindly eye noted the listless attitude of the young nun. She was seeking for someone to help Yvonne with the ailing peasants who were gathering in the cloister garth, and it suddenly occurred to the old sister that such occupation might be a change for Charlotte. She paused to look at the altar cloth, and praised the work, then added: " Put it away now for a time and come with me to the garth. There are several babies there, and you can help in keeping them amused while I attend to their mothers."

Charlotte readily obeyed and, carefully placing her valuable materials in the oak coffer allotted to her for the safeguarding of her cloth, she was soon among the patients.

Nanette Baptiste was there, her finger bound up; it was but a simple cut, but Nanette made every excuse possible for going to the convent, always hoping for the opportunity of converse with Yvonne; sometimes, but not always, it was possible. Sister Marie Gabrielle was well aware of the friendship between the two girls, and often managed to send them to the herb garden to gather something for her, so giving them the chance for a talk. Then Nanette would say eagerly: " Tell me something more about the good Lord Jesus, please, Mademoiselle."

And Yvonne told her all she knew.

" How I wish I had a Bible, as the Duchess had," Yvonne said one day. " I can remember so little, just the few stories she told me, and especially the story of the Cross; but there must be much more if only we could have some of the stories read to us instead of the legends of the saints, which I don't believe."

"But we know enough to love Jesus, don't we?" Nanette said simply; "and my mother and father love Him too. I have told them all you have told me."

"I am glad of that," Yvonne replied.

But on this particular morning Yvonne was too busy to be spared and Nanette saw she would have to go without private conversation.

Charlotte was among the mothers, talking to them and their babies. One young woman held a charming child of about ten months. The mother looked frail and the baby was heavy, nevertheless her eye rested with proud affection on her little son when she saw that he had attracted the attention of the young nun, as Charlotte held out her arms invitingly and baby responded with a crow and a chuckle. He smiled in a delightful manner, showing two pearly teeth and clutching at Charlotte's flapping cap, then putting two clinging baby arms round her neck, nestled his downy head close to her.

The touch of those baby hands was more than Charlotte could stand. An intense longing for children, for wee, helpless, confiding babies, was never long absent from her thoughts, and now all that the life of renunciation must mean for her swept like a surging billow over her mind, and with a choke in her voice she turned to Yvonne, exclaiming, "Take him, take him! I can't stand it."

Yvonne took the child wonderingly, and Charlotte disappeared.

As soon as she was free, Yvonne sought her friend, first in her cell, but she was not there, then in the garden; and at last in the old tool-shed, sitting on an upturned basket, Yvonne found Charlotte, her face swollen with weeping.

" Dear heart, what is the matter ? " Yvonne inquired tenderly.

Charlotte clutched her friend and buried her face in Yvonne's apron, but she did not answer.

" Tell me, dear one," Yvonne said, as she pushed off Charlotte's cap and passed her hand soothingly over the bowed head. " What has upset you so ? "

" The baby, the dear, precious baby. Oh, Yvonne, why should I who have a mother-heart be thrust into this life ? It's cruel, cruel ! Those baby fingers, those sweet, wee feet nestling in my hand as I held him ! And did you see that look in the mother's eyes of pride and affection ? Why, Yvonne, I'd rather be a peasant woman in a little cottage getting my husband's meals and nursing my baby than be as I am. What care I for royal blood in my veins ? What is it to me that my father says I shall one day be Abbess here ? It is home and little ones I want."

Yvonne scarcely knew what to say. How could she comfort poor Charlotte ? Suddenly she remembered what Charlotte had told her of the Duchess's conviction.

" Charlotte, your mother said she felt sure you would one day be released and yet become a happy wife and mother."

" Yes, she did, Yvonne, but how can it come

to pass ? Here have I been seven years, and you, ten years. Now we are women, for I am twenty and you are seventeen, and I ask you, from your experience of life in this place, can you see any possibility of release ? Who would dare help us ? We are not in touch with anyone outside who could or would lift a finger to assist us. My father would sooner see me dead."

" What about your sister Frances and her lord, the Duke de Bouillon; did you not say that they are Protestants ? "

" Yes, I think they are. Mother said that Frances had accepted the truth, but I know nothing much of her or her husband. Frances married when I was tiny, and Jeanne and Louise, my two other sisters, are in convents. No, there is no hope nor help for me, Yvonne."

Yvonne was silent for a time, then she said, " There is help for us—— "

" You are thinking of Henri de Valois and his promise to you as a child," Charlotte interrupted.

Yvonne smiled.

" No, dearest, not Henri. As a child and even as I grew older I cherished the idea that Henri would rescue me, but of course now I am grown up I see the unlikelihood of such a happening. Henri has probably forgotten. He must have many interests now; perhaps he is married, or, at any rate, betrothed. No, I do not look to Henri, but I do look to God; He is able to deliver us as He delivered the men in the burning, fiery furnace."

" You always loved that story, Yvonne," Charlotte said. " How I wish God were real to me as He is to you, dearest; but I am so cold and hard, so miserable, too—sometimes I feel desperate—I could scream and shriek as I did that day when the Abbess would not allow me to go to my dying mother, but I learned the futility of rebelling then. I yield now, but my heart rebels. How I hate this system, this cloistered life, this petty round of worshipping images and relics, in God's Name, too? Is it any wonder that some go mad? I believe I shall, too, some-day."

"No, no, dear heart, you must not talk like that. Oh, if only you knew the peace of trusting God, the loving Heavenly Father. Charlotte, do, do seek Him."

Just then the clanging of a bell warned the girls that duty called them. Charlotte rose with a listless air, and together the two friends left the garden, Charlotte assuming the calm air of composure which was becoming habitual to her in those days. Much care and thought were being given to her training, for it was well known that those in authority expected her to fill a high position in time in that princely and wealthy establishment, the convent of Jouarre. The result of her education and discipline was evident in the self-control which seldom failed her. Yvonne had never seen her so moved before, as she had been that morning by those little clinging arms. Charlotte as a rule scorned to show her real self, but could those whitewashed walls of that little cell where she slept have told a tale, they would have borne witness to many a heart-broken sob and much anguish of spirit in the dark hours of the night.

CHAPTER XII

TIDINGS FROM THE OUTSIDE WORLD

SISTER MARIE AGATHE, who ruled in the kitchen
of the convent, was in a dilemma. Not a new-laid
egg in the place, and now that the Abbess was
old and feeble she must have an omelette made
of new-laid eggs for her supper every evening.

" Dear, dear," Sister Marie Agathe exclaimed
as Sister Marie Mathilde reported that not a hen
was laying; " dear, dear, woe is me, there is
naught else will suit our lady but one of my most
delicious omelettes and a little white wine for
her evening meal."

" Would not a breast of a chicken nicely
roasted with a little bread sauce serve her for
once ? " Sister Marie Mathilde suggested.

" Tut, tut ! our lady will have what she fancies,
and that you know right well. The only thing
to be done is for you to get off to one of the
farms and bring me some eggs. Mère Baptiste
might have some, although we know eggs are
scarce now; but find some you must, owever ar
afield you have to go."

Sister Marie Mathilde, being a lay-sister, was
free to leave the convent for necessary errands,
and she prepared to go, albeit somewhat un-
willingly. The roads, or what answered for
roads in those days, were but muddy paths, and
now in the winter days Sister Marie Mathilde
knew she would find it heavy going. Within an

hour or two she returned, reporting that Mère Baptiste was away from home, but Nanette would come along presently with some eggs.

" And why did you not bring them, I should like to know ? " Sister Marie Agathe inquired. " Too lazy to carry a few eggs, I suppose."

" No, sister, I assure you it was not that; I am not lazy, but Nanette had but one egg, and she said she would go round the outhouses and see if she could find some more and then bring them along. I knew you must have three for our lady's omelette, and Nanette was very willing to bring them, so I thought it wise not to wait while she looked for the eggs."

" La, la ! I should think the world was coming to an end if you could not find some excuse for for yourself, and Nanette only wants to get along here to see if she can have speech with Mademoiselle Yvonne. There is great friendship between those two. But there, I'm not surprised; from the time that Mademoiselle came here a frightened little orphan she has never made friends with the other young ladies: they all seem to be down on her, so a little affection from Nanette has meant a lot to her."

" I can tell you why those two are so thick," Sister Marie Mathilde replied, lowering her voice; " they are both Protestants. Mademoiselle Yvonne has always been one, and she's taught Nanette to believe as she does herself."

" Tut, tut ! " said Sister Marie Agathe, " you know too much. You had better hold your peace; let the poor children alone to believe what they will, but don't talk about it; you

G

don't want to bring a hornet's nest about their ears."

"You're as bad as Sister Marie Gabrielle; she knows what Mademoiselle thinks, but she would do anything to shield her. La ! if Mademoiselle has no friends among the young ladies, with the exception of Mademoiselle Charlotte, she has a good friend in Sister Marie Gabrielle."

"Tut, tut !" again said Sister Marie Agathe. "Do get to work and cease your chatter. Our lady won't thank you for your talk, but she'll be swift to complain if the meals are not to her liking. Get on with the paring of the vegetables for the pottage."

Thus admonished, Sister Marie Mathilde silently set to work for a time, but presently, apropos of her own thoughts, she remarked: "I hear in the village that there is a fine fuss being made about religion nowadays. The Queen-Mother, the King, and his counsellors are set on stamping out heresy. In the big towns lots of Protestants are being threatened. I shouldn't be surprised if the Baptistes don't get into trouble; they rent their fields from our heads here and maybe they'll get turned out. Father Benedict is complaining that they don't come to mass or confession. La ! what fools folk are to get themselves into difficulties over such a little matter as religion. Now, what I say is—— "

Sister Marie Mathilde stopped abruptly, for Sister Marie Agathe raised her long wooden spoon threateningly with: "Get on with your work and cease your clatter, girl, or I'll—— "

For some reason best known to herself, Sister

Marie Agathe preferred not to have heresy, Protestantism and such matters discussed in her domain.

Not many hours later Nanette arrived with four new-laid eggs which the hens had obligingly laid, and, having been refreshed by Sister Marie Agathe with a delicious bowl of broth, the like of which Sister Marie Agathe often told her helpers no one could make as she did, Nanette left the kitchen; but instead of leaving the convent precincts immediately, she lingered in the cloisters, hoping for a glance of Yvonne. All was still, however, and the cloisters deserted, but after a time a bowed little figure came gliding along and Nanette recognised Sister Marie Gabrielle. She curtsied low and kissed the hem of the nun's robe while Sister Marie Gabrielle murmured a blessing. She was every bit a nun at that moment, but immediately afterwards, as she glanced at the winsome face upturned to her, her womanhood asserted itself and her kindly, understanding old heart knew without inquiry what Nanette wanted.

" Mademoiselle Yvonne is busy in the still-room, my child, and if thou hast time to spare she will welcome thy assistance for an hour; then the bell will ring for vespers and, if you wish, you may join us in worship."

" I fear, sister, I must return home then to get my father's supper, for my mother is away, but I can spare an hour to help Mademoiselle."

Sister Marie Gabrielle smiled. " I thought as much, my child," she answered, and Nanette sped to the still-room, where she found Yvonne alone, busy preparing a decoction of betony, ginger, honey and sage for medicine.

The two girls were delighted to find themselves without supervision—a most unusual thing.

" How clever you are," Nanette remarked, as she watched Yvonne at work. " 'Tis wonderful to me how much the sisters here all know. I suppose it comes of being able to read books."

Yvonne smiled. " Yes, and we younger ones have been kept pretty strictly to lessons."

" And you can read ? " Nanette queried.

" Yes. My own language, some English, and a little Latin."

" Oh-h-h." Nanette was much impressed.

" This concoction I am now making is taken from an English manuscript written more than a hundred years ago by a very clever naturalist. ' Take betoyne and sauge and synsburium, of eche y-liche moche—— ' " Yvonne paused and laughed. " I am forgetting you do not understand the language."

Nanette joined in the laugh, and then asked, " What else do you make here ? "

" Sister Marie Gabrielle makes wonderful waters —peppermint, rose, and lavender," Yvonne replied, " but her cordials are the best of all. She makes for our Lady Abbess and visitors, hippocras. It is made of rosemary, sweet marjoram, cinnamon, and ginger soaked in white wine and then passed through a jelly-bag, and finally it is added to new milk. And then we do distilling, for which we use this alembic; it is a slow process, but results in many useful medicines, as well as scents and toilet requisites."

" 'Tis wonderful," said Nanette. " You are all so clever; and to think you can read English. Would you like to go to England, Mademoiselle ? "

" I don't know. It is not much use my thinking of such a thing. What makes you ask that, Nanette ? " Yvonne inquired.

" I'll tell you. There was a pedlar in our village a few days ago, and he told father much news. He said that persecution for heresy is breaking out in our land, but in England, where it used to be so terrible under a Roman Catholic queen, it has now ceased, for they have a Protestant queen called Elizabeth, and I can't help wishing we were all there in that land. Father Benedict is getting particular about everybody being present at the celebration of mass. He has not insisted on father and mother coming, for he knows we have always been slack about religion, and he does not realise that we are Protestants, but if he gets to know it there may be danger for us."

" Oh, Nanette, do you mean that your father and mother have come to Christ and found in Him a Saviour ? "

" Yes, Mademoiselle, I do. I have told them all you have told me, and we pray every day to the Lord Jesus. We do not seek the aid of St. Joseph or the Mother of our Lord."

" I am glad. How I wish I could remember more of what the Duchess taught me; but I was small then, and yet I know the Holy Spirit keeps things in my memory—the really important truths—but I wish I had a Bible."

" A Bible ! " Nanette repeated wonderingly.

" I remember you mentioned that to me before. What is a Bible ? "

" That is the name of the Book the Duchess had. She said it was God's Book and that it contained His message to us all. I know that it had lovely stories in it."

" If it is God's Book for us all, I wonder why it is we know so little about it ? Was hers the only one, do you think ? " Nanette asked.

" No, I have heard that there are several. I sometimes wonder if there is one in the library here, for it contains some wonderful books; but I am not on duty there, so I don't get the chance of looking."

"Perhaps you will some day," Nanette replied, and then added, " I must not stay longer, for my mother is away, and I must get father's supper."

" Where has your mother gone, Nanette ? " Yvonne asked.

" Well, before she married she lived at the château of M. de St. Barbe, and sometimes she has gone there for a few days, because her aunt is maid to Madame de St. Barbe; and now the young lady, Mademoiselle Rénée, is to be married, and mother has gone to help in the festivities. It is to be very grand. Mother will tell me all about it when she returns. Mademoiselle was betrothed quite a long time ago, but she has been ill and the wedding was postponed. But she is well again now, and the wedding is to take place next week."

" And who is the bridegroom ? " Yvonne asked carelessly.

" He is called M. de Valois. He is a brave soldier and very handsome, so my aunt said when my mother was last at the château a year ago. Oh-h——— "

Nanette broke off in concern, for Yvonne had turned white and stood clutching the table for support.

" You are feeling faint, Mademoiselle. This room is too hot for you. Do sit down."

Nanette put her arm around Yvonne and gently forced her to sit on a stool.

Yvonne tried to smile. " Don't be alarmed, Nanette. It is only that I was so surprised to hear you speak of M. Henri de Valois; I used to play with him when I was small. He was such a nice, kind boy. So he is to be married next week." Yvonne sighed. But the decoction on the fire threatened to boil over and she had to hasten to the rescue. Presently she replied to an anxious inquiry from Nanette: " I'm all right now; it was only for a moment that I felt queer."

" You're sure ? " Nanette asked, " for I am afraid I must go now, and I can't bear to think you feel ill, for "—she hesitated, and then said, with her words tumbling out in a hurry—" I do love you so much, for if you had never told me of the Saviour I should never have known of His love and how He lives. I feel now that I can hardly look at the big crucifix in the church, although I do rejoice that Jesus died for me; but when I look at that form on the Cross I shudder, then I look up and remember He is not on the Cross now, but living above and caring for us down here."

" How glad I am that you love Him so,

Nanette," Yvonne said.

"I do," Nanette said simply, but with real earnestness in her tone. "I really must hurry now," she added.

Yvonne glanced out the window at the gathering dusk.

"I'm afraid it is nearly dark. Do you mind going alone?"

Nanette laughed. "I shan't be alone, Mademoiselle. Pierre Dupois promised to meet me."

"Oh-h-h. Did he—— ?"

Yvonne tried to think of something suitable to say, but Nanette broke in, thinking she knew what Yvonne was going to ask.

"I think he will be, Mademoiselle. I'm telling him all I know about the Saviour, and Pierre loves to hear."

So with a happy smile Nanette tripped off and Yvonne stood pondering. The blissful dream of her childhood days of the possibility of a rescue by Henri had, of course, faded more or less as she grew older and realised how unlikely such a thing was to happen, and yet—in her subconscious mind—there must have lingered some faint hope, for she felt now as though someone had dealt her a cruel blow. And Nanette, pretty, winsome Nanette, had gone off with dimpling smiles to meet her Pierre, while she, Yvonne, was imprisoned behind these massive walls, doomed to a life—a long life it might be—spent largely in the observance of monotonous, tedious ceremonies, a life unnatural in its seclusion and in its preclusion of the possibility of wifehood and motherhood.

The tears gathered in Yvonne's eyes as she absent-mindedly began putting away her utensils and restoring order in the still-room, ere the bell for vespers should ring. Her heart was sad, then suddenly her thoughts flashed back to the day when as a little child of seven years she had stood in the Duchess's boudoir. She seemed to see once again that kindly face bending to meet hers, and to hear the gentle voice saying: " Remember, Yvonne, Jesus Christ the Saviour is ever with you. He can help you when all others fail."

" All others may fail me," Yvonne said to herself, " but Jesus never will."

Yvonne was comforted, and as the bell rang out on the still evening air Yvonne hastily took her place in the procession of sombrely robed nuns as they moved with silent tread and gliding motion to the chapel. There was a look of quiet happiness upon her face that did not escape the notice of the keen eyes of the Abbess. It caused that lady a faint suspicion, a slight wonder, and brought Yvonne into observation, which was not likely to make for her well-being.

CHAPTER XIII

FATHER BENEDICT was seated in close confab with the Abbess. There were many matters on which they had taken counsel. The Lady Abbess, although of great age and in spite of the fact that she had been so long shut away from the world, still took a keen interest in matters of national importance, especially in the religious controversy which was so much to the fore just then. Priests and Roman Catholics in general were working themselves up to a high pitch of zeal and antagonism against the Huguenots. Montmorency, Condé, Coligny, were names much in evidence, but at the moment open warfare had not commenced. The Huguenots were too strong a body to submit tamely to persecution. There was little doubt that if they were not allowed to worship God according to the dictates of their conscience and the Word of God, although unwilling for bloodshed, they would certainly take up arms in self-defence. But their foes were wily and, with great secrecy, preparation was on foot for the extermination of the Huguenots in one great effort.

After discussing this fully, Father Benedict gave the Abbess an account of the struggles in the Netherlands, where the Prince of Orange was fighting an unequal contest with Philip of Spain, seeking to deliver the Protestants of that

land from the horrors of a ruthless persecution.
Judging from Father Benedict's way of stating
the case, William, Prince of Orange, was a rebel,
a dangerous fanatic, and great merit would
accrue to the one who was zealous enough to
rid the world of such a wicked person, with
which sentiment the Abbess heartily agreed.

Having discussed matters of importance in
the land and other countries, Father Benedict
turned his attention to things within the convent
walls.

" I wish to speak to you of a little matter in
connection with one of your nuns, which has
come to my notice, and about which I think it
will be wise for you to make an inquiry. Sister
Marie Madelon, in her confession to me, recently
made a statement which roused my curiosity,
or shall I rather say, my concern and interest.
She spoke of the temptation to belittle the Host;
she actually wanted to know why we said that
behind the jewelled doors of the shrine lay the
Christ. I inquired who had put such ideas into
her mind, and insisted on a full confession. I
had some difficulty in getting her to disclose
what had led to this perplexity in her thought,
and only when I threatened severe penance did
she yield to my demand."

" She is an obedient girl as a rule, and has
never given me any trouble," the Abbess
remarked.

" It is not of her that I wish to complain. She
made a full confession. It seems that when she
was in the chapel with Sister Marie Theodosia—
by the by, I believe this girl was obstinate and

trying as a small child. Was not her worldly name Yvonne d'Arande ? "

" Yes. She had been under the influence of the Duchess de Montpensier, whom we all know was a heretic, but she seems docile now."

" Ah, I fear not. Well, as I was saying, when the two girls were in the chapel, having been appointed to clean the brasses, Sister Marie Theodosia passed and repassed the tabernacle without making obeisance, and when Sister Marie Madelon protested, the wretched girl said, ' I cannot worship that which was made by the hand of man,' referring, of course, to the holy wafer."

The Abbess exclaimed in horror.

" I fear, Father, I may have been somewhat slack in my dealings with this girl. She has been much with Sister Marie Gabrielle, who, as we know, is apt to be lenient with the young. Sister Marie Gabrielle has always reported to me that the girl is obedient and tractable, and I have left it at that. I punished her when a child for rebellion in the matter of offering prayer to the blessed Virgin Mary, but since then I have not had much to do with her. In such an immense building as this, with such a large community, one girl can pass unnoticed."

Father Benedict did not say what he was thinking—that the Abbess was getting too old for her work—and the old lady continued: " I have given much time and thought to the instruction of others of greater importance, especially to the daughter of the Duke de Montpensier, who is developing well. I broke her

will when she had been here only a few months,
and subsequent events have proved that I was
wise in my dealings with her."

" Well, now that I have drawn your attention
to this state of affairs, I will leave the matter in
your hands. It is of the utmost importance that
such a thing should be dealt with immediately,
for it savours of heresy. And as a noxious weed
must be rooted out of a garden or an out-
break of plague cleansed by drastic measures,
so must such an evil doctrine be put away
from us lest it spread. If the girl refuses to
listen to reason, you will know how to resort to
sterner measures. Make her to understand there
is nothing before her but to yield to your wishes
or perish."

The Lady Abbess's stern old face with its skin
like parchment, dark hard eyes, and thin lips,
looked grimmer than ever as she replied: " You
need have no fear, Father. I am old, but my will
is law here, and I shall have no hesitation in
crushing that foolish girl, if necessary. She will
bend or break."

The old lady clenched her fist with a significant
gesture as though poor Yvonne was an insect
in her grasp.

Father Benedict soon took his departure, and
the Abbess sat in meditation pondering how
best to deal with the matter in hand.

Presently she rose from her seat in her usual
quick, decisive way and rang her bell. The next
moment she sank back in her chair with a short
gasp; a grey look spread over her face, and she
pressed her hands to her chest. Ah, that horrible

pain ! More than once lately she had been seized with a sudden spasm of agony lasting only a few moments.

Now, when a nun entered in response to her bell, she could only say briefly, " Call Sister Marie Gabrielle," and when that sister appeared, she was greatly concerned at the look of suffering on the Abbess's face.

Sister Marie Gabrielle administered a restorative and insisted on the Abbess retiring for the night. She was somewhat surprised that the Abbess yielded the point without argument. More than once during the night Sister Marie Gabrielle crept quietly into the Abbess's sleeping apartment to see if her aid was needed; however, the Abbess slept peacefully and in the morning was apparently herself again, and she wasted no time before summoning Sister Marie Madelon to her presence. Sister Marie Madelon was a simple-hearted girl who would not designedly have got another girl into trouble, but now she had revealed what Yvonne had said. Being of a timid disposition, she was too afraid of punishment for herself to conceal what she knew. So the Abbess easily got details of Yvonne's conduct and speech not only on that particular occasion, but she found that more than once Yvonne had given expression to what the Abbess termed rank heresy.

The Abbess's face was fierce as she dismissed Sister Marie Madelon and sat pondering as to what form of punishment should be meted out to Yvonne did she prove obdurate.

Meanwhile Yvonne, all unconscious of the

storm gathering for her, was again holding converse with Nanette. Yvonne was longing to hear details of Henri de Valois' wedding, and she guessed that Brigette Baptiste would have returned from her visit to the château of M. de St. Barbe, and so Nanette would have all the news to pass on; but for the tidings she was to hear Yvonne was totally unprepared.

As soon as the two girls could get alone in the garden, Yvonne said: " Do tell me what your mother said about the wedding."

Nanette looked at her companion a trifle wonderingly. Yvonne had never shown much interest in the happenings outside the convent precincts, but now her voice was eager.

" Oh, Mademoiselle, it was terrible and yet— but there, I'll tell you. The wedding never took place at all."

" Why ever not ? " Yvonne interrupted.

" Mother said there was a shocking upset the day before the wedding was to have taken place. Captain Henri de Valois told the bride's father that he was a Protestant, and M. de St. Barbe is such an ardent Roman Catholic that he was furious and refused to allow his daughter to marry Captain de Valois."

The colour came and went in Yvonne's face. Then Henri was still free; the thought brought joy to her heart, but only for a moment. How foolish she was, what difference could it make to her ? Henri had, of course, forgotten all about his little friend of years ago. She sighed and gave her attention to what Nanette was saying.

" It was awful. Mother said her heart ached

for the poor young gentleman, for, when his father heard of his confession, he declared he was no son of his and disowned him on the spot."

Nanette's explanation was somewhat involved, but Yvonne understood what she meant, and Nanette continued: " Mother said he was so brave, so calm, but he left the château alone, with bowed head, just cast off by all."

" Poor Henri ! I told you I knew him when I was small, didn't I ? "

" Yes, Mademoiselle. Mother told me that he is such a tall handsome soldier now. I do hope he will marry some nice Protestant girl some day; but he will be quite poor, for his father has disinherited him. It was terrible, and mother said the old M. de Valois looked ten years older than he did when he arrived at the chateau with his son. Although he seemed so stern, yet he must have been fond of his son, for he seemed broken-hearted; both he and Captain de Valois looked stricken. Mademoiselle Rénée de St. Barbe cried and scolded everybody, and her father raved and stormed while Captain de Valois begged his father not to cast him off."

" Oh, I am glad he was brave and made confession of his faith. I wonder if he, too, is the fruit of the faithful teaching of the Duchess, as I am."

" The Duchess," Nanette repeated. " I remember you told me she was the mother of Mademoiselle Charlotte and that she was a Protestant. Is Mademoiselle Charlotte one, too?"

Yvonne lowered her voice to a whisper. " I don't know, Nanette. Charlotte isn't happy. I sometimes fear she knows only the truth in her mind but not in her heart, and that Christ Jesus is not a reality to her; but I do pray for her—won't you pray too, Nanette?"

Nanette was about to reply, but a young nun came hurrying to meet them, that is, hurrying as fast as her long, heavy, woollen frock would permit. As she reached the girls she said to Yvonne: " You are to go to the Abbess at once. My, I believe you are in for a scolding, from what I heard her say to Sister Marie Thérèse. I wouldn't be in your shoes for something."

Yvonne hastily bade Nanette " Good-bye," and made all speed to obey the summons. It would never do to keep the Abbess waiting; and as she went she wondered innocently what could be the cause of this sudden demand for her presence.

CHAPTER XIV

FOR CHRIST'S SAKE

FAR down underground in a damp, dark dungeon Yvonne lay. Just how long she had been there she did not know, for part of the time she had been unconscious, and it was almost impossible to distinguish night from day in that dimly lit spot. Too sore to move, for the flagellum wielded by Sister Marie Thérèse's muscular and willing arm had done cruel work, Yvonne could only lie uneasily on the bed of straw where she had been placed after the punishment which had followed her interview with the Abbess. At first she had been too dazed for consecutive or clear thought, but as the days passed slowly, broken only by a visit daily from Sister Marie Thérèse bringing a portion of rye bread and a flagon of water, Yvonne's mind began to act once again and she recalled the details of that conversation which the Abbess had held with her. Yvonne shuddered at the remembrance of the threats held out to her if she refused to comply with the wishes of the Abbess. She required that Yvonne should make obeisance in front of the shrine where lay the consecrated wafer, and also offer a prayer to the Virgin Mary.

Weak and suffering much pain, for a time Yvonne wondered what the end of this contest would be. She felt in despair. Would it be imprisonment in that dark dungeon until death should come to release her, or more cruel torture? The Evil One whispered: " You are too young to suffer and to die. God will understand if you yield outwardly; your heart can still be true to Him. When Sister Marie Thérèse comes again, tell her you will do what the Lady Abbess wishes."

It was an hour of great temptation, all the more so that Yvonne knew so little of the Bible. Very few actual Scripture words were known to her, only those which she had learnt as a little child; during her sojourn in the convent she had been taught far more of the legends of the saints than the pure Word of God. But in spite of her ignorance the Holy Spirit could and did speak to her.

Just when the darkness in her soul seemed deepest, when she felt forsaken of God and man, a Voice sounded in her soul: " Will you deny Me, My child ? I who suffered such agony for thee ? "

Tears filled Yvonne's eyes, and she cried aloud, " O Saviour, strengthen me to bear. Thou knowest that I love Thee and would not willingly deny Thee, but I am weak indeed, and I am afraid I shall yield."

Once again the story that had so thrilled her as a child came back to her memory with fresh power, and she whispered: " O Lord, Thou art with me here as Thou wast with those men in the burning, fiery furnace."

Joy such as she had never experienced before filled her soul, the dungeon became holy ground, a consciousness of the Presence of the Master was very real, and presently she fell asleep and slept as calmly as a little child in its mother's arms.

No sound from the outside world or from the convent penetrated to that dungeon. Yvonne knew nothing of what was happening that night. Footsteps hurrying here and there, doors opening and closing, and presently towards dawn the summons to every inmate to rise and pray for the soul of the Lady Abbess, for not long after midnight the angel of death had entered, and she who had so long wielded supreme authority there, whose word had been law, who brooked interference from none, could not disobey the call that came; massive doors and stone walls could not keep that intruder at bay, and the Abbess's earthly day was over, the place filled by her for so many years was vacant, and the nuns whispered to each other in awe-struck tones, " She's gone," devoutly crossing themselves, even as they said it.

Low, mournful chantings filled the chapel, and apparently all were plunged into woe; but, alas ! the head of that convent had ruled by fear, and, with few exceptions, a feeling of relief filled every heart, and at once many were occupied with the thought: " Who will be her successor ? "

For the time Sister Marie Gabrielle, as the eldest nun, took charge, and if there were some who thought, because of her gentle, kindly manner, they would be able to take their own way, they found themselves mistaken. Her rule, if kind, was firm and wise, and the routine of the convent was uninterrupted save for the extra time given to prayers for the soul of the departed

Abbess and during the days of ceremony and ritual which immediately followed her death.

One of Sister Marie Gabrielle's first actions was to repair herself, accompanied by Sister Marie Agathe, to the dungeon where poor Yvonne lay. The Abbess had concealed from Sister Marie Gabrielle exactly what discipline she had meted out to Yvonne. She only knew that Yvonne was in disgrace and had been condemned to solitary confinement, and now, as she flung open the door of the dungeon, she exclaimed in horror as she saw Yvonne lying prostrate and wan on her bed of straw.

Yvonne started and trembled as the two women entered. In the dim light that filtered through the bars of a minute opening she could not see who they were, and her first thought was that she was to receive some fresh torture; then, with a gasp of relief, she recognised the kindly, wrinkled old face of the nun she had learnt to love, and she tried to struggle to her feet.

It was not long before Yvonne was lying on a bed in the sick-room and Sister Marie Gabrielle applied healing, cleansing lotions to her wounds.

" Dear, dear ! " the old nun said, " a day or two more of neglect and these wounds would have been poisoned and the child's life not worth a pin."

How heavenly it seemed to Yvonne to rest in that quiet sunlit room; it seemed like a dream, and she feared she would presently awaken to find herself back on that bed of straw in that horrible hole where the rats had held carnival each night.

"Why had the Abbess consented to this change of treatment?" she wondered, and presently she asked Sister Marie Gabrielle : " Has our lady given permission for this?"

"My child, our Lady Abbess departed this life at two o'clock this morning. God have mercy upon her soul!"

The old nun paused a moment in her task of rolling a bandage to cross herself and murmur a few prayers, counting her rosary as she did so.

"Oh-h!" Yvonne gasped in astonishment. "Then God has delivered me from the burning, fiery furnace."

Those were peaceful days for Yvonne lying there in the sick-room, cared for so tenderly by Sister Marie Gabrielle. As she grew stronger, Sister Marie Gabrielle encouraged Yvonne to talk freely, and Yvonne was delighted and surprised to find the old nun so desirous of hearing all she could tell of the simple Gospel teaching which she had learnt long ago.

Sister Marie Gabrielle sometimes dropped the knitting that usually kept her fingers employed, and gave all her attention to what Yvonne was saying.

"Ah, my child, if only I could believe it for myself. A free and full forgiveness for sin. I'm old, very old. I forget for the moment exactly how old. Let me reckon. I came here in the year 1501, when I was sixteen, and it is now 1569. What does that make me, Yvonne?"

Yvonne calculated and said, " Eighty-four, sister."

Sister Marie Gabrielle's eyes grew dreamy,

her thoughts were back in the past.

" Yes, Louis XII was then on the throne. He was a good king and called the father of the people, but his early marriage was a sorrowful affair. Joan, a cousin of the king, daughter of Louis XI, was chosen for him before he was old enough to know his own mind. As soon as he was his own master he divorced her. Poor Joan, she was broken-hearted. She, so young and innocent, retired into a convent, where she remained all the rest of her life. Dearie me! These arranged marriages so often mean grief for one or the other. And here am I outliving so many of my contemporaries. Ah, those old days! There was my friend Francis, and—" she broke off and sat musing; after the fashion of the aged she was back in the memory of her far-away youth.

Yvonne waited, and presently Sister Marie Gabrielle said: " What was I saying, child? "

" You were speaking about your age, sister. You told me you were sixteen when you came here," Yvonne said gently.

" Yes. Sixty-eight years have I dwelt in this place, and every day I have had one aim in view, to so live and act that I might acquire merit, that I might lessen the years in purgatory for my soul. And now what you tell me makes me fear all this has been done in vain—all I have suffered has gone for nothing. Holy Mother of God, help me to understand, plead for me to thy Holy Son."

The old woman lifted her hands appealingly to Heaven.

" Sister," Yvonne spoke a trifle timidly; she

had suffered so much for her belief that even with Sister Marie Gabrielle she was not quite sure how far she might express herself freely. " Sister, will you not come straight to the Lord Jesus ? One of the Bible words that the Duchess made me learn as a child I remember distinctly : ' There is One Mediator between God and men, the Man Christ Jesus,' so we may come to God by Him."

There was silence in the sick-room for a time. Yvonne was praying earnestly for the old nun whom she loved so dearly, who had been so unfailingly kind to her all through the dreary days of girlhood spent behind those prison walls.

Presently Sister Marie Gabrielle rose. She laid a gentle hand on Yvonne's head—it was the nearest approach to a caress she ever allowed herself— and said, " Thank you, my child, for your words. I will seek Christ, but it is difficult for one so old as I am to change her views. I am so afraid it will be presumption on my part to approach Him without the mediation of saint or angel, I must, oh I must find rest for my soul, if it is to be found anywhere, for I am full of fears as I know my time to depart must be drawing near, and I am afraid—so afraid," her voice sank to a whisper: "What is there beyond?"

" Sister, God can take away all fear. He will, if you trust Him and Him only for salvation. Just let your meritorious life go and take salvation from Christ."

Sister Marie Gabrielle's face was very gentle and the sunken eyes shone as she stood looking at Yvonne.

" Ah, my child, you have crept into my heart. I fear I am wrong in loving you as I do, for I promised God when I was only sixteen to love Him only, renouncing all earthly love, and I meant to do it, yet as the years have passed I have found it so difficult. I have not loved Him as I should have done. I have tried, oh, how I have tried ! I have disciplined myself, I have fasted, I have prayed, but love—ah, love is not easy. I have found it a simple matter to love you, little one, but God has seemed so far away, and yet, if God is not to be found within this sacred building, where—where can He be found ? "

Sister Marie Gabrielle's voice was very pitiful, a broken-hearted cry that reached the ear of the ever-compassionate One above, who knows every seeking soul, and as Yvonne said simply, " Sister, God loves you, and is seeking you," the words thrilled the old nun's soul as she turned away. No longer was her mind occupied with the tormenting accusation of her lack of love, her efforts to win salvation, her own meritorious actions, her self-righteousness; but the Holy Spirit made real to her soul something of the wondrous love God had for her, and as the days passed the salvation procured on Calvary at such a cost became a reality, and rest was obtained at length for her weary soul.

CHAPTER XV

THE NEW ABBESS

NATURALLY there was much thought in the minds of the inmates of the convent as to who was to be the successor of the departed Abbess. Discussion on the matter was not permitted openly; nevertheless the younger ones found many an opportunity of speculating among themselves on the question.

Would it be Sister Marie Gabrielle? No, they decided—she was too old. Sister Marie Thérèse was suggested. They felt they must expect stern discipline if it came into her hands. Maybe it would be someone from another convent. No one among the novices could tell, but it was noticeable that Charlotte de Bourbon said little but that did not mean that she was not thinking much about it. She recalled her father's prognostication before she entered the convent that she would be Abbess in time, for he had the power to ensure her being appointed. Charlotte had no desire whatever for the responsibility; still she was exceedingly capable, had administrative faculties, and in considering the possibility of her being raised to the position so coveted by some, she felt the rule would be better in her hands than in some others. Her keen sense of justice and her early training made her determine that there should be no religious persecution under her regime, should she be called upon to take control. Her indignation at Yvonne's treatment had been intense, and when Sister Marie Gabrielle allowed her to sit with Yvonne for a short time, she had been full of sympathy for her friend.

Although to the younger members of the convent it was a matter of speculation as to who would be their future Abbess, the older nuns knew what to expect. Was not Charlotte de Bourbon of the royal blood of France, and had not her father great influence in ecclesiastical affairs ? They could all have given information on the matter had they so wished.

One day Yvonne ventured to remark, " Sister, I do wish you were going to be our Abbess," and she was surprised at the answer she got.

" My child, I am too old, for one thing; it needs someone with more vigour than I possess to control this large establishment, with its many inmates. Have you no idea on whom the choice has fallen ? " the old nun asked.

" No, indeed. Is it someone here ? " Yvonne inquired anxiously, as she rapidly reviewed in her mind some of the older nuns from whom she was likely to receive scant sympathy, She dreaded a renewal of persecution at their hands.

She was speechless with amazement for a moment or two when Sister Marie Gabrielle announced, " Your friend Charlotte is to be our Abbess."

" Charlotte ! But surely she is too young."

" It is not considered so by those in authority and although she is young she is certainly better fitted for the work than many older women. I have great respect for her steadfast character and well-balanced mind. Of one thing I feel sure, Yvonne—religious toleration will be practised under Charlotte's administration. But here she comes, and I will leave you two together that you may hear from your friend what she thinks of her new responsibility."

Yvonne glanced somewhat shyly at Charlotte, wondering if this fresh turn of affairs would make any difference in their friendship. Charlotte's face was gloomy. She was by no means elated by what her father considered the high honour placed upon her.

" Yvonne, have you heard ? " Charlotte asked.

" Sister Marie Gabrielle has just told me, but I see you are not pleased."

" Pleased ! Is it not just a tightening of my bonds? Father writes that I am greatly favoured, that my position is one of greater importance than that of a princess, that my reward will be not only reverence and respect in this world but certain glory in heaven; but, Yvonne, it's my own fireside, home life, a husband, children that I crave ! "

Charlotte flung out her hands as she spoke, a gesture expressive of the emptiness of her heart and life.

" Poor Charlotte ! " Yvonne murmured.

" I am remembering my mother's prophecy," Charlotte continued, " that some day I should be liberated and the desire of my heart given me; but does it—I ask you—does it look like it ? I am more hopelessly bound than ever."

Yvonne hesitated. Then something other than

her own imagination prompted her to speak and she was amazed at her own words, " Charlotte, I believe, I have the conviction that somehow, some day, you and I will both be free. God has a plan for our lives; I don't believe this iron-bound, cloistered existence is His will for us."

"Oh, I don't know, Yvonne. God seems so far away. I wish I felt like you do, dear heart; you seem to know God in a way that is difficult for me to understand, and mother was the same. How weary I am of this constant repetition of prayers to the Virgin Mary, to the saints, this telling of our beads, genuflexions, and fastings, it is all so empty. And as for holiness here ! Look at the petty jealousies, the bickerings, and selfish ambitions for chief places among us. Do some of them think that I do not see through their intentions when they flatter me and pay me attentions not given to others ? It is only because they have long thought that the position of Abbess would be mine, and so they wish to obtain my favour."

" Well, anyhow, Charlotte, it is an immense relief to me to know you are to be our head. I know how just your rule will be, and, oh, when you know the Lord Jesus as your own Saviour you will be able to teach others about Him. Charlotte, just think what opportunities will be yours. I'm going on praying for you, and the answer will come."

" I certainly need your prayers, Yvonne," Charlotte replied gravely, " for great responsibility will be mine."

CHAPTER XVI

A GREAT DISCOVERY

CHARLOTTE was at work in the library, an immense room containing priceless manuscripts. She had now been ordained Abbess for some weeks. Her appointment had been inaugurated with due observance and ritual, very impressive to all those who were to be in her charge; nothing had been lacking to give importance and spectacular glory to the ceremony as befitted the appointing of the daughter of the Duke de Montpensier to such high office in the Church. Now the convent had relapsed into its ordinary routine. Some had wondered whether the new Abbess, because of her youth, would be able to maintain order in so large an establishment; but speculation soon ceased, Charlotte proved herself exceedingly capable—no slackness was tolerated, her rule was firm, just, and impartial. She was bent on doing her duty, but there was a weary droop at times in her attitude when alone and a sad expression in her eyes. It was an unnatural life she was living. Of an active disposition, the confinement was ever increasingly irksome to her. How often she thought of the wide expanse of her father's park, of the horse she had delighted to ride, of the exercise she missed so sorely, until at times the bitter ache that took possession of her seemed intolerable.

One of the duties she had undertaken gave her

pleasure. The library had been somewhat neg-
lected latterly, and Charlotte was determined to
revive the interest of the nuns in the collection
of manuscripts, which was of considerable size for
those days. With this aim in view she was steadily
working through the shelves, selecting those
manuscripts which she considered would be
suitable for the novices and younger nuns to
read. On the morning in question she had just
taken down a large volume, a manuscript beautifully illustrated and written, the work of some
skilled scribe. Every capital letter was in itself
a thing of beauty—the colouring was superb and
the script clear and firm.

Charlotte's eye fell on some familiar words
and her attention was caught. She read page
after page, and when at last she paused she
exclaimed to herself, " How delighted Yvonne
will be ! This is the same Book that mother
possessed from which she read to us; it is a
Bible."

Her impulse was to rush off and find Yvonne;
but remembering her office, and realising that
such a hasty action would be lacking in dignity,
she rang her bell and set a message to Sister
Marie Theodosia, requesting her attendance.

Yvonne promptly arrived and Charlotte im-
parted the news of her discovery. Yvonne's eyes
shone and her cheeks flushed. Here was joy
indeed, and together the two girls bent over the
precious volume and read some of its words.

" Charlotte," Yvonne at last exclaimed, " will
you read this aloud to us all ? Oh, do; it will bring
light to many in this house if you do. Let us

give it its right place, and honour it, for it is God's message to us."

" I wonder if it will bring light to my poor heart," Charlotte said musingly. " Certainly I will read it I will appoint a time when each day we shall gather and listen while one reads aloud."

Yvonne was overjoyed, for her heart was hungry for the Word of God; all she knew was so precious to her, and now the chance had come to learn more. The teaching the Duchess had given her had been kept in her memory by the gracious Holy Spirit, but it was but limited.

Charlotte, too, was keen; so day by day, at her command, the nuns gathered and listened to the reading, with varying emotions—some with indifference, some scornful, but many with eagerness and a receptive spirit.

Just at that time the Protestants of France were making an effort to get various tracts giving Gospel teaching into the various Roman Catholic religious houses, and a packet was sent to Jouarre. Charlotte received them with much interest, especially when she found they were written by Martin Luther, of whom she had heard in her childhood days, and she studied them carefully and then read them to others. These were wonderful days for her. All she read brought back to her memory her mother's teaching, which had not greatly impressed her at the time of receiving it. Vividly she recalled the large Bible from which the Duchess had read, her mother's tears and prayers, the written protest; she lived over again those happy days

of youth, and with a heart burdened and sorrow-
ing she found her way to the Cross, and there
entered into the blessing of salvation, With her
new-found joy transforming her whole outlook,
Charlotte earnestly sought the salvation of those
in her care. She taught nuns that they must
not hope to win heaven by their own merit,
salvation was by grace alone through faith in
the finished work of Jesus Christ, to the merit
of which they could not add. Prayers to the
Virgin Mary and to the saints were given up,
acts of adoration before the crucifix or shrine
were abandoned, and Scripture teaching was
given to all in the convent and to the peasants
who came for aid in their troubles. Nanette and
her mother were present as often as possible, and
both rejoiced in their privilege of hearing God's
Word read.

All this was good, but both Charlotte and
Yvonne felt that their position in a Roman
Catholic convent was irregular, but what could
they do ? They often discussed the difficulties
of the situation and their longing for freedom,
but escape seemed impossible.

One day Charlotte had been reading the
account of Peter's imprisonment and of his
miraculous escape. It was the first time either
she or Yvonne had heard the story, and it
brought encouragement to their hearts.

" God could open our prison doors, Charlotte,
as He did for Peter," Yvonne remarked when
the two were alone.

" Yes, I know He could. It will have to be a
miracle, but I will not doubt His power. Of

J

course it seems, humanly speaking, impossible·
My father would sooner see me dead than allow
me to return home, of that I am convinced."

"And I have no home nor relations," Yvonne
said sadly. Then after a pause, she asked, "What
about your sister Frances? She and her husband
are Protestants, could they not give you a home"

"I don't know; I might bring disaster upon
them if I fled, Oh dear, I often wish I belonged
to a less important family—there is no obscurity
for us. Yvonne, have you noticed that Father
Benedict is growing suspicious? He is asking
questions, and I fear we have those among us
who will betray us. I feel almost sure that he
suspects that I and others have abandoned the
Romish faith and accepted Protestant teaching.
If so, and it is reported of us, there will be dark
days ahead for us, or for me at any rate."

"And for me," Yvonne said firmly. " If you
are called to give an account of your views, then
I must declare myself one with you, and others
here will do the same, I am sure—dear old Sister
Marie Gabrielle for one. Isn't her childlike faith
and joy delightful ? "

" Yes, indeed. But how terrible if one so old
and feeble should be called to suffer. We know
that persecution is being carried on. Father
Benedict told me only yesterday that war is
raging between the Huguenots and Catholics.
He said the Catholics are gaining victories everywhere, but one can't be sure of the truthfulness
of his report. I asked many questions, but was
guarded in what I said."

" You feel he is suspicious ? " Yvonne asked.

" Yes, I am sure of that. He was trying hard to trap me, pretending to be very communicative. He told me how the war started. Of course, for long it has threatened to break out, and not long ago a pretext was found for beginning. At a place named Vassy the Protestants were holding a service in a barn, when they were discovered by the soldiers of the Duke de Guise, who was travelling through the place. These soldiers were very insulting and a tumult arose; the Duke came on the scene and received a blow, and one of his soldiers at once killed many of the Protestants. Father Benedict said, ' in self-defence.' "

" And it has not ended there? " Yvonne asked

" No, I think not, but we have so few means of getting reliable information. Father Benedict only told me all this, I believe, to see if I should express sympathy with the Huguenots. He was crafty enough almost to pretend that he was on their side, but I was not to be drawn. He felt baffled, I think, but only for the moment; he will return to spy out more."

Yvonne sighed. She had been so happy lately. The sympathetic atmosphere created by Charlotte's attitude to the truth, the joy of knowing that several of the nuns had accepted Christ as their Saviour, and the sweet simplicity of Sister Marie Gabrielle's faith had been sunshine to her soul, and now they were threatened with fresh troubles, renewed persecutions—it may be with death itself.

Charlotte put her hand on Yvonne's shoulder with an affectionate gesture.

"God won't desert us, Yvonne. Remember how Peter's prison door opened."

"Yes, and if we are called to suffer for His sake, He will give grace, of that I am sure. I was wonderfully helped when I was in that awful dungeon, Christ was so real to me, and if persecution should come to us again, He will sustain."

Charlotte agreed, and after a pause she said, "We won't meet trouble half-way. Maybe our loving Heavingly Father is planning some good thing for us. I don't forget the assurance my mother had that my prison door would open, and do you remember your childish confidence that Henri would rescue you?"

Yvonne laughed. "Of course I have grown out of that. I wonder what he is doing. I suppose he may be fighting in this horrid war. How wonderful it is that we three who learnt from your mother of Christ are all His now!"

"Yes, indeed. Mother's prayers have been answered."

CHAPTER XVII

CIVIL war was raging in France. The inhabitants of many a small town and village were exposed to all the horrors of fire and sword. Towns were taken and retaken, and the history of small battles, sieges, and massacres would fill many volumes. The Prince of Condé had seized Orleans and established the chief seat of his party there, and published a manifesto calling on all good Protestants to assist him in the cause. They then applied for assistance to the Queen of England, and offered to put the town of Havre into her hands as a requital for the succour which she engaged to send them. In 1569 the Catholics gained a great victory, the Huguenots being defeated in the battle of Jaurnac; but the Huguenots, although for the moment beaten, were far from being subdued, and under the indomitable Admiral Coligny rallied again and again. The Duke de Guise aimed at the entire suppression of the Huguenots but they were a strong party, possessed of about a hundred fortresses, castles, and cities, and in spite of persecution and massacres they held their ground.

Early in 1570 Admiral Coligny won a victory for them at Arnay-le-Duc, the result being that a treaty was signed, the Huguenots gaining favourable terms, and for a time the religious warfare ceased.

Scant tidings of all this reached the Abbess and nuns in the convent of Jourre, Peacefully the days passed, amd they were more concerned just then about the rapidly increasing frailty of Sister Marie Gabrielle. Always busy and active, attending to any who came to the convent for aid or those who ailed in the house, still making her lotions, ointments, and physics, it was difficult to get her to rest. But there came a day when the old nun was obliged to confess her inability to rise from her couch. So thin and wasted she was, her form barely showing under the coverlet as she lay on her low bed in the bare cell she had occupied so many years; small and square, with whitewashed walls, a tiny window set high so that it gave no outlook, a stone floor, the bed and a stool the only furniture, it was silently eloquent of the life of suppression which Sister Marie Gabrielle had practised from early girlhood. She, whose childhood had been spent in luxurious surroundings, rooms tapestry-hung, down-cushioned chairs, silken garments, dainty food, from these Sister Marie Gabrielle had turned aside in her youth with one thought, that being to win salvation. Now, in her old age, her eyes had been opened to see her mistake; salvation had been won for her by the atoning work of the Saviour.

One day in that last illness Yvonne sat beside the aged nun, her hands busy with her distaff and spindle. On the walls of the cell hung a large crucifix, and it was significant that the stone floor was slightly dented immediately beneath that figure of the Christ. How it spoke of the long hours of agonising vigil to which those silent walls could have borne witness had they possessed the power of speech.

Sister Marie Gabrielle's eyes were fixed on the crucifix. Presently she spoke. " Yvonne, my child, do you think you could remove that ? " She pointed with trembling finger.

" Remove it ! " Yvonne repeated with wonder in her tone.

" Yes, I do not want my mind to be occupied with a dead Christ. I am realising that He lives, that His life is mine as His death was for me. Oh, if only I had known this years ago, how different my life might have been."

" But you have lived for others, sister," Yvonne said, with the desire to bring comfort to Sister Marie Gabrielle's mind for there was a note of distress in her voice as she spoke of her life.

" Yvonne, it might look like that to you, but I know it was selfish. Everything I did was from one motive—to earn my salvation and lessen the pangs of purgatory."

Yvonne was silent, for she knew not what to say, and again Sister Marie Gabrielle said, " Take the crucifix down, my child."

Yvonne rose to her feet; she hesitated, she was not accustomed to acting on her own initiative. " Shall I ask——" she began.

Sister Marie Gabrielle smiled. "Yes, we must not forget we still have a Lady Abbess. Charlotte seems such a child to me I am apt to forget her office, but go and ask her, dear."

So Yvonne found her friend and came back with full permission to do what the old Abbess would have considered an act of sacrilege.

Next day Charlotte visited the cell and brought with her a piece of parchment an which she had inscribed with beautifully illuminated lettering the words: " I am He that liveth . . . behold I am alive for evermore."

She hung it on the wall where before the crucifix had hung, and a ray of morning sunshine filtering through the narrow window caught the gold of the letters and it shone forth with brilliance. It seemed to transform the cell from a place of gloom and tears, which it had been, to a place of light and glory.

Sister Marie Gabrielle smiled with great pleasure. " Child," she said, " that is just a picture of my life—all gloom and fear formerly, now changed to sunshine and glory as I trust my Saviour."

Each day found Sister Marie Gabrielle weaker; the nuns one and all loved to be with her—she who had nursed so many a sick one was now tenderly cared for. It was evident that she was just slipping away. One evening Charlotte and Yvonne were sitting quietly with her, Sister Marie Gabrielle had been dozing; presently she stirred, and Yvonne rose to give her some barley water, for her lips looked parched and dry, but the old nun shook her head, and the girls waited.

" What was that you read, Charlotte ? " the words came slowly with great effort, " about —never—see—death ? "

Charlotte pondered a moment, and then said,

" Do you mean the words ' If a man keep My saying he shall never see death ' ? "

" Never see—death."

The dying woman made an effort to lift herself. Yvonne slipped her young strong arm around her, amd Sister Marie Gabrielle rested against the girl and the room was very still.

Then slowly the words came, " I have lived in fear of death all my days, and now— now—I know that for the one—who trusts in Christ—it is true—never see death. I see—my Saviour. It is just His—call. Yes—Lord—I—come to be— with Thee."

The words were whispered, and the two girls had to strain their ears to catch the broken sentences. Sister Marie Gabrielle's head drooped on one side, and the watchers saw that the earthly life was over, and life, the true full life, had begun.

At that moment Sister Marie Thérèse pushed open the door of the cell and, seeing what had taken place, she asked in a whisper, " Shall I call the nuns to pray for her soul ? "

Charlotte spoke firmly. " Certainly not, sister. Sister Marie Gabrielle's soul is with Christ. We have no need to pray for her."

Sister Marie Thérèse turned away muttering to herself, " Father Benedict shall hear of this; it is rank heresy, as sure as my name is Thérèse. It shall be reported to those who will know how to deal with the matter."

CHAPTER XVIII

THE SIGNS OF A COMING STORM

SISTER MARIE AGATHE moved about the big stone-paved kitchen with an abstracted air. Her hands were busy, peeling apples, whisking eggs, pounding spices, but she worked mechanically. A close observer would have noticed by the look in her eyes that her thoughts were not in her work. The last year or two had brought a great change to Sister Marie Agathe. She was a simple-minded woman, and had lived for the larger portion of her life accepting the doctrines she had been taught, the religion in which she had been reared; but when Charlotte de Bourbon began reading the Bible to the nuns, including the lay-sisters, of whom Sister Marie Agathe was one, Sister Marie Agathe had drunk in the good news like a parched land absorbing a gentle shower. She heard, she believed, and the knowledge of salvation through the atoning work of the Lord Jesus brought joy to her soul. There had always been an undercurrent of anxiety as to whether she was " making her own salvation," although she was of too placid a disposition and too busy to let the thought weigh her down to any great degree; but now as she learned to pray to her Father in heaven, through Jesus Christ and in His Name, her trust was very real, and her gladness found expression in many a simple word of testimony.

From the first day of the arrival of Charlotte in the convent Sister Marie Agathe had taken an interest in the little lady of royal blood, and now that Charlotte had led her into the Light, the lay-sister's devotion to the Lady Abbess was great, and thoughts concerning her lady's welfare were causing Sister Marie Agathe much anxiety. Her assistant, Sister Marie Mathilde, was a person possessed of an inquisitive mind; she had an almost uncanny way of finding out things that other folk would not have discovered. There was very little that happened in that convent of which Sister Marie Mathilde did not know. Observant to a degree, quick of hearing, and with sharp eyes, she seldom came into the kitchen without having some information to pass on. As a rule Sister Marie Agathe took little heed to what Sister Marie Mathilde chose to tell her. If it were true that one nun was jealous of another, or such a one was becoming careless in the matter of genuflexions, or another was evidently hankering after a worldly life, Sister Marie Agathe would murmur, " Well, I never ! " or " Dearie me ! " and serenely continue her work. But recently Sister Marie Mathide had brought news that had caused Sister Marie Agathe to question her very closely.

" Good lack, here's a pretty story," Sister Marie Mathilde had said as she came into the kitchen.

" What now ? " Sister Marie Agathe inquired indifferently. She was stooping over a big fire, over which hung a huge cauldron from which came a savoury odour; she added a sprinkling of powdered herbs before she straightened herself to listen.

Sister Marie Mathilde glanced round to see if they were alone ,and lowered her voice to a whisper. " I've had my suspicions lately that Sister Marie Thérèse was up to something, and I've been watching. So this morning when Father Benedict left the Lady Abbess's room and Sister Marie Thérèse waylaid him, looking so meek, with downcast eyes and hands folded over her cross, and asked if she could have speech with him, I says, says I to myself, ' 'Twould be just as well if I found out what that old cat is up to now.' "

" I'm ashamed of you, sister," Sister Marie Agathe said.

" You wait a bit. You'll be glad I've found out what I have. Forewarned is forearmed. Well, I kept out of sight till I found out where Sister Marie Thérèse would take Father Benedict. They went into the refectory, which, of course, she knew they would have to themselves this time of the day, and closed the door. I thought to myself, thought I, ' 'Twould be just as well if I did a bit of weeding to that flower-bed under the refectory window,' which I happened to know was open. So round I slipped and started my job, keeping close to the house so I couldn't be seen from inside."

" That's where you've been, you hussy, neglecting your duties in the kitchen all this time."

Sister Marie Mathilde giggled. Sister Marie Agathe's scoldings never disturbed her in the slightest.

" You listen. I didn't hear the beginning of their conversation, of course; but I heard enough to know that Sister Marie Thérèse is accusing our dear lady of heresy. I heard that old cat say, ' Lutheran doctrines are being instilled into the innocent and unsuspecting minds of our nuns.' But there, I can't remember all she said, and sometimes, sharp as my ears are, I lost a sentence or two; but I know Father Benedict is going to carry the report to the bishop or even it may be to the Pope himself, and our lady will be dealt with."

Even placid Sister Marie Agathe was aroused by these tidings, far more so than she allowed her informant to guess; but Sister Marie Mathilde saw that for once she brought news to the kitchen that was gaining the attention of Sister Marie Agathe. She felt quite elated, and proceeded to give her own views on the matter.

" I'll tell you what's at the bottom of this. Sister Marie Thérèse is wild that so young a woman has been appointed Lady Abbess. 'Tis jealousy that's at the root of this. She thinks if she can oust our lady from her position and curry favour by reporting the heresy, she might step into our lady's shoes. La, la ! What times we should have here. Our old lady's rule was severe enough, but 'twould be mild as milk in comparison with what this creature would do."

" Well, Sister Marie Thérèse ought to be accustomed to our lady by now; she's been Abbess two or three years," Sister Marie Agathe replied.

" Oh, that sort bides her time before she strikes. I know what 'tis, now that dear old Sister Marie

Gabrielle is dead Sister Marie Thérèse is the eldest here, and, my word, she hates it like poison having to submit to our lady's rule. Well, 'twill be some excitement for us if Father Benedict reports, as he will, no doubt."

" Oh, stop your chatter, woman, do," Sister Marie Agathe said, roused by her anxiety out of her usual calm. "Who is Sister Marie Thérèse, I should like to know, thinking there could be any chance of her being appointed Lady Abbess ? The idea of such a thing ! "

" Well, you never know. Sister Marie Thérèse has got the ear of Father Benedict."

But Sister Marie Agathe refused to listen any further, and insisted on Sister Marie Mathilde getting on with her work. But the conversation was exceedingly disturbing. Sister Marie Agathe pondered much. She knew only too well the reality of the danger that menaced the Lady Abbess. Many in high places were suffering persecution for their faith, and what would be the fate of their dear lady were she called upon to give an account of herself and her belief ?

Sister Marie Agathe was right in thinking that for one holding so high a position in the Roman Catholic Church, for one of princely blood to declare herself a Protestant openly, would rouse the ire of both ecclesiastical dignitaries and royal personages as well as her father the Duke de Montpensier.

Was there anything she—humble woman as she was—could do to help ? Sister Marie Agathe's brain moved slowly, but after meditating for a few days on the matter she determined to seek an interview with the Lady Abbess and give her warning.

One evening after Charlotte had been reading the Bible to the entire community, Sister Marie Agathe lingered, while the others trooped off to their various duties. Agitation made her cheeks red and her heart thumped as she stood, a hesitating figure, in the doorway. She was just wondering how to proceed, when Yvonne, noting her hesitancy, said gently, " Sister, is there anything the matter ? Can I help you in any way ? "

" Oh, Sister Marie Theodosia, could you ask our gracious lady to allow me to have speech with her, and you too, if you will be so kind as to listen ? "

Yvonne at once turned back into the room and told Charlotte of Sister Marie Agathe's desire and soon they were closetted together behind closed doors in Charlotte's room.

Sister Marie Agathe told her story, and both Charlotte and Yvonne were extremely grave.

" I am not surprised," Charlotte said. " I have long been conscious that we are in two parties here, and although some are rejoicing in the Reformation doctrines, some are antagonistic; but what am I to do ? "

" Charlotte, couldn't you escape before it is too late, and things get worse ? " Yvonne said earnestly.

" But where could I go ? I know my father would not receive me."

" Your sister Frances—surely you could go to her," Yvonne said.

" I can't feel that it would be right for me to

run away. Oh, how I wish I could have some sign from God. If some circumstance arose which would cause our doors to be opened, I should feel I was being guided. I am remembering how when God meant Peter to leave his prison the doors were opened for him; he didn't climb out some window, or make his own plans for escape. I think it must be right for me to stay here for the present; surely if God means me to leave He will give me some definite guidance."

Both Yvonne and Sister Marie Agathe begged her to consider whether she could not quietly slip off to her sister in some disguise, but Charlotte felt convinced that it was not the right thing for her at the moment.

" How could I leave you all ? Some ardent Roman Catholic would be appointed in my place, and those of you who believe the truth would suffer. No, sister." she turned to Sister Marie Agathe and placed her hand on the lay-sister's shoulder with a kindly gesture, " you must not fret, but pray much that we may be strengthened, and if we are to suffer persecution, that we may be strong in the Lord to bear for His sake."

Sister Marie Agathe's rosy face grew pale at the thought, and she gave a suspicious little sniff.

" Oh, Lady," she said, " I'd give my life to save you if I could, for I can never forget that if it had not been for your teaching my soul would still be in darkness. You have led me to the Saviour."

Charlotte was deeply moved at Sister Marie Agathe's confession, and she said, " To God be the glory, sister. I value your love, and some day perhaps you may be able to help me. Who shall say what I may need in the days which lie ahead, for they look dark indeed ? "

" Dark, yes, if it were not that He who is Light is with us. My experience in that dark dungeon made me realise that when things seem blackest then it is that His Light shines the brightest. I feel now I would not have been without those dark days, for I learned to know a little of what God could be to a soul in trouble. It was like "—Yvonne paused for a simile—" it was like being a little child in all-enfolding arms."

" Underneath are the everlasting arms," Charlotte said softly.

"Oh, what lovely words ! " Yvonne exclaimed.

" I found them in the Bible only yesterday," Charlotte replied.

" Do show them to me. I did not know them," Yvonne requested.

So together they went to the library, where Charlotte turned over the leaves of the Bible and showed Yvonne the text.

Both girls rejoiced as one that findeth great spoil, for much of the Bible was absolutely new to them, and daily they explored its treasures and laid up God's Word in their hearts.

CHAPTER XIX

A RESCUER

CHARLOTTE looked grave indeed. A messenger had brought an imposing-looking document for her, which she was now reading. It was a notice that shortly a deputation of ecclesiastical dignitaries would wait upon her, and give her the opportunity of explaining the report that had reached the ears of those in authority that she was instilling Reformation doctrines into the nuns in her charge in the convent of Jouarre. The letter contained a barely concealed hint that unless she were willing to recant, or could give satisfaction that the report was a false one, severe penalties awaited her, witnesses would be called and the whole matter gone into thoroughly.

Just when the deputation would arrive Charlotte did not know, and she could only wait and pray. Yvonne, Sister Marie Agathe, and those who had embraced the Protestant teaching, believing the truth with their hearts, joined with Charlotte in prayer for strength and wisdom.

The days passed slowly as they waited with somewhat anxious hearts as to what might be coming.

Then one evening Nanette came in asking for an interview with the Lady Abbess. Her face was flushed and eager as she told her news.

" Oh, Lady, the soldiers are marching in this direction. Pierre Dupois has seen them only three miles from here."

" Which army ? " Charlotte inquired.

" The Roman Catholics, Pierre says. But the rumour is that the Huguenots are also gathering, and maybe there will be a battle quite near. Father says where more likely than on the common which surrounds the convent ? I felt I must warn you, Lady."

" Thank you, thank you, Nanette But I don't see there is anything we can do. Surely the soldiers will respect the sacredness of our building. Oh, how I wish I had someone older and wiser to advise me."

Charlotte felt the responsibility of her position pressing on her. Here had arisen an unprecedented circumstance: there was no prescribed rule by which she could be guided.

" But, Nanette, is it safe for you to be out, with soldiers in the neighbourhood ? You must not run into danger for our sakes," Yvonne, who was standing by, said.

Nanette glanced at Yvonne, and with eyes gleaming, she said, " I'd do more than that for you Mademoiselle. But I'm not alone; father is waiting at the gate for me, so I must not linger. Father and mother say if they can do anything for you, they will be only too glad to help."

Charlotte and Yvonne both sent messages of thanks and Nanette departed.

Charlotte summoned her nuns and told them the news, and then gave the order that each one was to retire to her cell and pray for guidance and protection.

Soon the shades of night fell, and the nuns,

all more or less in a state of apprehension, retired to rest. The query in all their minds was, what would the morning bring ?

Charlotte and Yvonne lingered together, and soon Sister Marie Agathe joined them, making an excuse for her presence by bringing a tray bearing bowls of savoury broth. Before separating for the night the three women—two of whom were so young, Charlotte being twenty-five and Yvonne twenty-two—knelt together and prayed. A simple little prayer-meeting; only the last few years had there been such in that religious building—no crucifix, no rosary, no mention of saint to intercede, only in the Name of Jesus they came " boldly to the throne of grace to obtain mercy and find grace to help in time of need."

Then separating, they sought their cells, and calm in the assurance of the Presence and care of the Saviour, they slept.

Not many hours of the next day passed before the noise of battle was heard. The once pure air was fouled with smoke, the song of birds was exchanged for shouts, cries, and groans, the grass, where a short time previously sweet wee daisies had lifted their faces to the sun, was now trampled into mud mingled with blood. The nuns shivered with fear as the battle raged outside their walls. Would the tide of battle pass and they and their dwelling be left unmolested ?

Toward the evening they were left no longer in doubt. The soldiers flung themselves on their doors, broke down walls, and began to swarm in, bringing in their wounded and demanding food. Hostilities had ceased for the moment.

Charlotte came bravely forward, and the general of the Roman Catholic army came toward her. Courteously he told her he must have possession of the convent for his men, but that he would send all the younger nuns, including herself, under escort to the nearest convent. Some of the older nuns could remain to nurse the wounded.

Charlotte thanked him and asked for a short time in which the nuns could get together anything they wished to take with them, and then they would be ready.

All was confusion. Charlotte sought to re-assure the nuns who were frightened, and briefly gave the necessary orders, calling the names of those who were to remain, while the general gave instructions that horses and wagons were to be brought in which to convey the ladies to safety. Every nun hurried to her cell. and Charlotte went to hers. She had no sooner reached her room when Yvonne joined her.

Speaking softly but eagerly, she said, " Oh, Charlotte, is not this the sign for which you prayed ? The doors are opened——"

Charlotte gasped. "Yvonne ! Are you thinking that too ? But where can we go ? '

" Mère Baptiste and her husbnad will give us shelter till we can make our plans. Let us slip away in the darkness and confusion, and make our way to their farm," Yvonne replied

" Do you know in which direction their farm lies ? Is it not two miles from here ? " Charlotte asked.

Yvonne was nonplussed for the moment. Not once had either of them been outside the precincts of the convent all the years they had resided there. The convent walls enclosed meadows, orchard, and gardens of some acres, and all exercise had been taken within those sheltering walls.

Yvonne suddenly brightened. "Sister Marie Agathe knows the way; she, as a lay-sister, knows the neighbourhood well. I will try and find her."

Noise and disturbance was all around them; the tramping of heavy feet, the groans of the wounded as they were brought in echoed and re-echoed—strange noises, indeed, to be heard in those erstwhile quiet corridors. Yvonne hesitated as to where to look for Sister Marie Agathe, but before she stepped from the shelter of the Abbess's room Sister Marie Agathe's rosy face peeped in.

She was delighted at the suggestion the two girls made to her, and readily agreed to lead Charlotte and Yvonne to the farm as soon as possible.

" Then," she said, " I must return—my place is here. It may be I can teach some of these poor wounded men to look to the Saviour. 'Tisn't a fit place for young things like you dear young ladies, for I don't like the way some of these officers are looking at the young nuns; but I am past my youth, and we elder ones can make ourselves useful. But if you need me to aid you in your escape, let Père Baptiste come to me with a message, and I shall be ready at any time."

" I must see the others off first," said Charlotte, and Sister Marie Agathe and Yvonne agreed, but planned that in the darkness Charlotte and Yvonne instead of getting into the wagons as the others did, were to slip off and wait for Sister Marie Agathe in the little stone hut in the herb garden.

A little later Charlotte and Yvonne, crouching in the shadow of an old yew tree, watched the wagons depart, and then silently glided away. Their movements were unnoticed as with beating hearts they trod the old familiar way across the terraced lawn, down the flagged path under the cypress trees, then beneath the rose pergola out on to the grass walk where the wind whistled and moaned in the trees, and Yvonne kept close to her friend, for was it not here that the ghost of a former Abbess was supposed to walk ? Yvonne was trembling with excitement; fifteen years had she been in seclusion, and now, now, was she to be plunged into the world ? What lay in front of her ? As far as she knew she had not a single earthly friend to whom she could turn, but her confidence was in God—He would not fail her, He would provide; but naturally emotion played a part in her feelings just then. Charlotte realised Yvonne's agitation, and, stronger woman that she was, she calmly whispered words of comfort.

A few yards more and the shelter of the potting-shed would be gained, when suddenly a harsh voice sounded in their ears.

" Where away, my dears ? Here, let's have a look at you. Ah, ah ! Two pretty lasses slipping off alone. That will never do; you need a protector, my dears. Come along with me. I shall know how to look after you."

The man laughed coarsely and the girls were terrified; nevertheless Charlotte pulled herself up and with dignity said, " Will you be good enough to go away. You have no right here; return to your captain."

"Ah, ah ! Well, pretty mistress, give me a kiss first and then I'll think about it."

He caught Charlotte by the wrist and put his jeering face close to her. Charlotte felt his hot breath on her cheeks. Yvonne seized his arm to pull him away; but the man was strong, and although both girls struggled they were no match for him. His rude, triumphant laugh rang out on the night air—and then, unexpectedly, he measured his length on the grassy sward.

Charlotte and Yvonne gasped. From whence had come this deliverance ? A tall form stood beside them, and by the light of a lantern he carried they saw their rescuer was a captain in the Huguenot army.

" Get off, you coward, and be sharp, or I'll run my sword into you," he said, addressing the prostrate figure at his feet.

The man rose, and, muttering to himself, slunk away, and the captain turned to the girls, who were both trembling.

" Can I assist you, ladies ? "

Yvonne swayed and would have fallen had not the new-comer caught her in his arms.

" Oh, Yvonne," Charlotte exclaimed, " don't faint."

"Yvonne!" The name awoke memories in the soldier's mind; but he said nothing, only looked around for a place of shelter.

"This way," Charlotte said, and led him to the potting-shed, where he placed Yvonne on a pile of sacks. However, Yvonne quickly revived, and Charlotte was relieved to hear her say, " I'm so sorry, Charlotte, I'm all right now."

" It was the shock, dear heart." Turning to the soldier, who stood by, she said, " How can I thank you for your timely assistance? That horrible man——" She paused, for the young captain was holding the lantern so that the light fell full on Yvonne's face, and then he abruptly turned to Charlotte.

" I believe——" he began, when Yvonne interrupted with a joyous exclamation. " Why, it's Henri! I know you by your eyes."

"And it is my little playmate Yvonne," Henri said. The words were simple, but the tone! The tone in which they were said was expressive of the feeling that lay behind the words. Charlotte felt the thrill and drew her own conclusion.

Then, turning to Charlotte, he said, " I knew I should find you here, but I had no idea Yvonne was with you in the convent of Jouarre, I was only a small boy when she was taken away, and if I knew where she had gone then, the name faded from my memory. But this is indeed splendid that I have found you just at the right moment. Now, tell me, have you any plans? Am I to conclude that it is your desire to escape from the bondage of the convent? I fancy it must be so, or you would have gone with the others in the wagons provided for them."

" Yes, yes," both girls exclaimed, and Yvonne added, " Charlotte and I are both Protestants, and we feel God has made the way of escape for us from the thraldom of a life into which we were thrust against our wishes."

There was no time to explain further, for just then the door of the potting-shed was gently opened and Sister Marie Agathe's kindly but anxious face peeped in. She started in amazement to find her ladies were not alone, but heaved a sigh of relief at the information Charlotte proffered.

" Sister, this is an old friend of ours," and Yvonne added, " God has sent him just at the right moment." Then, turning to Henri, she continued, " We have not had time to plan much. Sister is going to take us to some Protestant people we know who have a farm about two miles from here. We are sure of shelter there until we can form some plan for the future."

" My idea is," said Charlotte, "for us to disguise ourselves and get to my sister Frances."

" I think we had better hasten, for we must not be about after daylight," Sister Marie Agathe broke in, and Henri agreed with her, only adding that he should accompany them. Sister Marie Agathe led the way with Charlotte, and Henri and Yvonne fell behind. Henri's strong arm supported her, and although their walk was accomplished almost in silence, for they were mindful of the saying, " Hedges have ears," and they dared not betray their whereabouts and destination to anyone, yet both felt blissfully happy.

Speaking in a whisper, Henri explained his presence in the neighbourhood. It was as Yvonne had already surmised, he was fighting in the Huguenot army.

" We must have a long talk before long," Henri said as they drew near the farm. " Do not make any plans until I come to you. I must hasten back now to my men, but at the first opportunity I will come. God bless and keep you, little Yvonne ! "

" He has done so, Henri, all these years, and He who has kept will keep."

So they parted, both with hearts aglow.

CHAPTER XX

A WARM welcome was afforded to the fugitives from the Baptiste family. They made light of the apologies offered for rousing them at such an hour. Nanette was highly elated at being honoured by such visitors; Brigette Baptiste busied herself by preparing beds for Charlotte and Yvonne in the upper room, while Nanette coaxed the smouldering log-fire on the hearth into a flame and heated milk for her guests. Brigette's motherly eyes soon descried that both Charlotte and Yvonne were extremely fatigued. The strain, shock, and excitement, as well as the sleepless night and unaccustomed walking exercise, had tired them; so their kind hostess insisted on their going to bed, and, as she shrewdly remarked, " It won't do for you to be seen, my dear young ladies. The quieter you are the better, both for your health and your future plans, so just have a long sleep, and when darkness falls again then we can gather in the kitchen and talk things over."

After partaking of some refreshment Sister Marie Agathe started back for the convent, and at early dawn Charlotte fell asleep, but not so Yvonne. The events of the last few hours had been so wonderful, so unexpected, that she felt almost dazed. Her heart was filled with thankfulness, and she saw how her Heavenly Father

had been working for her, bringing Henri de
Valois right to the spot just when she so sorely
needed a friend. How amazing it all was ! Only
two days before and life was passing in the
convent in its usual routine, and now everything
was changed. She and Charlotte were free from
their bondage, and although thoughts of the
future had been awesome a few hours ago, the
arrival of Henri on the scene had tinged everything with a roseate hue. At last, after prayers
for the future and praise for the present wonderful deliverance, Yvonne too fell asleep, and the
day wore away while they slumbered.

About five in the evening they awoke, and,
with the bouyancy of youth, they had regained
poise and lost all sense of fatigue.

They talked quietly together for a time before
venturing to descend the ladder which led to
the living-room below. They found Brigette
Baptiste alone; Nanette was busy with her
father on the farm, milking at that hour being
in progress.

It was a glorious evening in the early spring of
1572, and the birds were carolling their evening
song of praise, and through the open doorway they could see one of the fairest scenes in
beautiful Normandy. So long accustomed to the
convent grounds, bounded on every side by high
walls, the stretch of country, fields intercepted
by woodlands, entranced them.

Brigette Baptiste rose at their arrival and
made a humble curtsey, then hastened to find
them seats. She would have remained standing,
but both girls protested.

"We want to consult you about our future, and how can we talk comfortably if you are not seated?" Charlotte said, and Yvonne added her persuasions. So Brigette yielded, and, after inquiring how they had slept, settled herself to listen to their plans, or rather Charlotte's, for Yvonne was unwilling to take any steps for the moment, although she said nothing just then.

"My idea is that we disguise ourselves and get to my sister Frances and her husband, the Duke de Bouillon. They are both Protestants, and will, I hope, give us shelter while I write to my father. I hardly dare hope that he will give me his protection and a home, and yet I long for his approval and my old home. Frances will doubtless plead for me, and Yvonne, where I am, I am sure you will be welcome. You will come with me, won't you?"

Charlotte turned to Yvonne as she spoke with the winsome smile that made her so attractive. Now that she was free from the shackles which had bound her, her face had lost its expression of gravity and care. She was willing to face the future with dauntless courage and faith in God.

Yvonne hesitated before she answered, and Charlotte threw out her hands with an expressive gesture.

"Oh, Yvonne, I could dance all round the kitchen in my joy that I am no longer the Lady Abbess of Jouarre. I'm just Charlotte de Bourbon. I'm free, free! I feel I can face anything. I'm like a bird let loose from a cage."

Yvonne smiled happily.

"Yes, it's all so wonderful. I feel as though

I'm dreaming and shall presently wake up in my cell."

" Let me pinch you to make you realise that you are awake," Charlotte said merrily.

Brigette Baptiste smiled. She was glad to see the dear young things so happy, and yet her heart was full of forebodings as to what the future might hold for them. She knew that both girls had relentless foes, and their action in ignoring their vows and escaping as they had, would bring upon them the wrath of the Catholics as soon as it became known what had taken place.

However, she said nothing to damp their spirits, but remarked that her husband was saying that their neighbour, Miller Fontaine, would be taking a wagon-load of flour to Caen before long, and he, being a Protestant, would be willing to convey them as far as he went.

Charlotte and Yvonne listened, and the good woman continued, " You could hide in the wagon among the sacks while in this neighbourhood, and then, when farther afield, where you would not be likely to be recognised, you could travel openly, if you were dressed in peasant clothing."

" Capital ! " Charlotte exclaimed. " But, Mère Baptiste, neither Yvonne nor I have any money with which to buy clothes——"

Brigette Baptiste interrupted. " Lady, do we not owe you and Mademoiselle much? Mademoiselle Yvonne first taught us the way of salvation, and lately, by your reading the Bible to us, how much we have learnt. You are welcome to anything we can supply."

" Thank you," Charlotte said simply. She

saw that the kind woman meant every word she said. "Perhaps some day we shall be able to recompense you in some small measure for your kindness, but we shall never be fully able to do that. Yvonne," she continued, turning to her friend, " what do you say to this plan ? "

Yvonne had no desire to leave the neighbourhood and go to Charlotte's sister—not, at any rate, while Henri was in the neighbourhood, and until she had seen more of him, but she could not desert her friend. Charlotte could not travel alone, so she said, " Perhaps we ought to take this opportunity which is afforded by Miller Fontaine's wagon. I feel sure God will guide us, Charlotte."

" Well, we need not decide anything just now. When my husband comes in we will ask him if he knows when Miller Fontaine takes his next load to Caen," Mère Baptiste said.

" Meanwhile you must find us something to do; we can't be idle—can we, Yvonne ? " Charlotte remarked, and Yvonne agreed with her.

Brigette Baptiste protested, but the girls insisted, Yvonne adding, " I wish I could get to work in your garden; that is work I understand and like."

" You must not be seen outside in those garments, Mademoiselle. I am wondering if you would mind wearing some of Nanette's clothes. She has a good supply, as we have been spinning, weaving, and making in preparation for her wedding in a year's time."

" Spinning !" Charlotte exclaimed. " Now that is something I can do. Let me make a start."

"But first, please, change your clothes. We seldom get visitors here, in this out-of-the-way spot, but my husband and I both think it would be better not to run any risks."

So Charlotte and Yvonne returned to the upper room and, with a good deal of merriment, robed themselves in Nanette's garments.

The house possessed no looking-glass—only a highly polished piece of brass reflected somewhat distorted visions; but they could see each other, and each congratulated the other on the changed appearance, and they rejoiced in the feeling of physical comfort brought about by the discarding of the long, heavy, woollen dresses, and other cumbersome, unnecessary things.

Nanette's clothing, although quite simple, was becoming—home-spun, home-dyed, home-sewn. Charlotte was wearing a dress, golden-yellow, dyed from the agrimony plant, and Yvonne's was purple, dyed from an infusion of whortle-berries. She could scarcely remember having worn coloured garments before, and both she and Charlotte took a girlish pleasure in the change, and with joy laid aside the immense flapping stiffened white caps and spoke of the time when their hair should have grown. Not but what they both had pretty hair, although short. Yvonne's was curly, of a soft brown shade, in some lights almost golden; while Charlotte's was dark and straight but abundant, framing her face in a becoming fashion now that it was released from the oppressive cap.

However, the two girls did not frivol long. The condition of affairs both for themselves and others engaged in the terrible struggle was too serious to admit of their being light-hearted and careless for long, and presently as they lingered together in that upper room, their conversation became thoughtful, and soon they were kneeling in earnest prayer asking for guidance and protection for themselves, for victory for those engaged in the fight for right and justice, for reward for the Baptiste family for their great kindness in sheltering the fugutives, and then they joined the family downstairs with a great peace filling their hearts and the consciousness that all would be well.

CHAPTER XXI

THE DIVIDING OF THE WAY

HENRI DE VALOIS as he parted from Yvonne in the darkness of that eventful night was greatly stirred. He, as well as Yvonne, felt that he must be dreaming; he could scarce believe that he had found Yvonne at last.

The last two or three years of his life had been lonely and hard. True, he had many acquaintances but he felt being banished from his home keenly. He was a man to whom home must always mean much, and relations still more. He loved the old château in which he had been born and in which his boyhood had been passed, and he still loved his father in spite of the old man's anger and sentence of banishment. Henri could not believe that he was forgotten, and hoped that some day there would be a reconciliation, for he knew his father had always loved him sincerely. He felt sure it was not hatred of him personally, but bigotry and prejudice, that kept his father silent. He constantly prayed that his father might be brought into the Light and yet seek his son and restore him to favour.

The years that had passed since Henri's public confession of faith, which had brought about such a severance from his former life, had taught him much. His Christian life had developed, and he had found the reality of the Presence of the Master as he took his stand under the banner

of the Cross. He was known as a leader of the
Huguenot party, and there were those among
the Catholics who would have rejoiced had
Henri de Valois been slain in battle.

Henri knew that he was often in danger, and
up to the present it had not greatly concerned
him. However, his thoughts were not of these
things as he trudged along across the fields, down
muddy tracks, through copse and spinney in the
darkness, but a song of joy was in his heart, and
he whispered to himself, " Yvonne, my little
Yvonne, unchanged and as sweet as ever, I have
found you at last."

Then perplexing thoughts followed. Would
he find those years of sequestered cloistered life
had given Yvonne a different outlook on life
and make her shrink from, and unfitted for,
ordinary existence in the world ? She had seemed
to him in that brief interview like a timid child,
a frail flower that must be handled with the
greatest care and sheltered from life's breezes
which would only have a bracing effect on other
souls. He must go carefully. He longed to tell
her that all those bygone years he had cherished
the memory of the little child he had loved to
guide and protect in his childish fashion. He
wondered if, when he did tell her all this, and
that his love for her had grown with his growth,
would she be willing to marry him ? He tried to
recall just what she had said in the potting-shed,
but he had been so excited at that moment at the
discovery he had made that Yvonne's exact
words escaped his memory; but she had given
him the impression that she was not a Roman

Catholic. In that case she would not consider her vows binding—vows taken before she had come to years of discretion, words put into her mouth which she was too young to fully understand.

Then his thoughts turned to Charlotte. What would be the outcome of her escape? Yvonne d'Arande might possibly quit the convent and her action excite little comment in those stirring days; but Charlotte de Bourbon, daughter of the Duke de Montpensier, a prince of the royal blood of France, it was another matter for her, besides which—was she not the Lady Abbess? No doubt, if it became known that he had aided her in her flight, it would double the hatred already felt for him, and arouse great indignation towards poor Charlotte. Henri realised the gravity of the situation. The sooner she could be placed under the protection of Henri Robert de la Marke, Duke de Bouillon, the better, and what could he arrange for Yvonne? He thought long, and eventually decided, if the people at the farm were Protestants, and could keep Yvonne, it would be best for her to remain in seclusion until he could safely marry her, which should be at an early moment. His hopes soared. Oh, to have a home, however simple it might be, and a wife awaiting him whenever he was free from his work!

As Henri meditated happily a streak of dawn in the eastern sky caught his notice. A cock crowed in the distance, from bushes and trees just beginning to show a sprinkling of green the twitter of birds started, and a new day began, a day of hope, and Henri recalled the words: "This is the day that the Lord hath made, let us be glad and rejoice in it." He had passed through many days of sorrow, but now he lifted his heart to God in a paean of praise that there seemed to be a brighter pathway ahead. As soon as possible he wished for an interview with Yvonne, and, if she were willing, surely, for her safety and happiness as well as his own, it would be wise to marry at the earliest opportunity. Then he fell to planning for her future, for his calling must of necessity take him often away from her for weeks at a time; but he could find a snug little home, and he felt sure his old nurse Denise, with whom he still kept in touch, would willingly keep house for her loved young master's wife.

But Henri's walk was over and a busy day lay in front of him. He was in doubt as to whether warfare would be renewed; but both sides had suffered severely, and the leaders of the two armies had for the moment much to occupy them. The convent was filled with men, both Catholic and Huguenot, and the few elderly nuns left were busy indeed. Before night fell many graves were dug, and the lads from village or town homes laid to rest in the convent precincts. Mothers, wives, sweethearts sorrowed. Suffering followed in the train of the needless struggle caused by Rome's efforts to force all men to worship according to her false tenets.

The day passed and Henri had no opportunity of visiting the farm. Not until the evening of the following day was he free to wend his way to

the little home that gave shelter to the girl of
his choice.

He found Charlotte and Yvonne as well as
the Baptiste family gathered round the fire that
burnt cheerily on the hearth. Charlotte was busy
with her distaff and spindle, and Yvonne was
teaching Nanette a new and intricate pattern
in lace-making called " point-de-vise." It was
worked with a needle, and was just then much
in demand.

Henri was welcomed shyly. Charlotte seemed
the only one quite at ease in his presence.
Yvonne's eyes drooped and her cheeks flushed.
Soon they were all deep in conversation as to the
girls' future.

Good Jacques Baptiste reported that within
a few days Miller Fontaine would be making a
journey to Caen and would willingly do his best
for the ladies to give them a start on the way to
Charlotte's sister's home.

" But," said Henri, " is there no one else who
could accompany Mademoiselle de Bourbon ? I
think, if possible, it should be someone older
than Mademoiselle d'Arande, besides which I
want to suggest another plan for her."

It was quite usual in those days for a young
man to make a proposal of marriage publicly,
generally to the girl's parents or guardians when
she might or might not be present. When Martin
Luther wished to marry Katherine von Bora he
took with him three friends to the burgomaster's
house, where she was residing, and in their
presence sought her hand in marriage, the
ceremony taking place the same day. So no one

was unduly surprised when Henri said simply,
" I wish to marry Mademoiselle d'Arande, if she
is willing."

Nanette's eyes sparkled. Here was romance
indeed. However, Charlotte's face fell; she felt
a pang at the thought of being separated from
her friend. Brigette Baptiste smiled and nodded
her head to show her approval, while Yvonne
alternatively flushed and paled.

There was a moment of silence, then Charlotte,
dignified in manner as became the late Lady
Abbess, and unconsciously taking her position
as responsible for one of her nuns, turned to
Yvonne and asked: " Dear heart, is this your
wish too ? "

Yvonne looked up and caught Henri's eye. A
look of intense longing met her gaze, an expression of heart hunger. He said nothing, but if
ever a voiceless petition was made by one human
being to another it was at that moment, and
Yvonne replied to Charlotte: " Yes, Charlotte,
I do wish it."

Henri rose and gravely grasped Yvonne's
hand in his, as plighting his troth.

It might have been an awkward moment for
Yvonne had not Nanette exclaimed delightedly:
" Oh, Mademoiselle, I'm so glad. I've always
wanted this for you, but it seemed so impossible
when you were a nun."

Everybody laughed, and Charlotte put her
arm round her friend and kissed her, while
Yvonne exclaimed: " But, Charlotte, I am forgetting, I cannot desert you. I must go with you
on your travels and see you safely in your sister's

home before I think of my own happiness."

" There is no need for that," Charlotte replied. " Do you not remember that Sister Marie Agathe said if I needed her she would go anywhere with me or do anything for me. I am sure she would be willing to accompany me to my sister's home."

" And a much better arrangement," Jacques Baptiste said, speaking almost for the first time. He had been feeling awkward, simple man that he was, in the company of " grand folk," as he termed them, but he was exceedingly practical, and now he felt that he could make a suggestion.

" Sister Marie Agatha knows more of the ways of the world, she being a lay-sister, than either of you two young ladies, besides being a middle-aged woman. People will conclude she is Miller Fontaine's wife if she is dressed suitably, and you, Mademoiselle, if you don't mind, must be passed off as his daughter. 'Twould be a good idea if you could manage to do a bit of rough work the next day or two and coursen your hands a little, or that dainty hand of yours might betray you."

Charlotte was quite willing for this and said so.

Jacques then took the opportunity of asking Henri something of the position of affairs in France and in other lands, for he was an intelligent man.

Henri spoke gravely of their own dear country, and then said: " It is not only in France that there is warfare and persecution for those who seek to follow Christ. In Spain the Protestants are suffering great torture and in the Netherlands there has been wholesale massacre as well as many battles. You may have heard of William, Prince of Orange; he is fighting a brave fight against the King of Spain, pouring out his wealth on behalf of the persecuted, so far, I fear, with scant success."

" I remember hearing my father speak of him when I was at home," Charlotte said. " But I think he was not a warrior then, simply a wealthy, generous man."

" Yes, that would have been so, for it was about the year 1560 that Prince William espoused the cause of the Protestants in Netherland. You were then in the convent, were you not ? " Henri asked. Then he continued to tell his listeners more of the prowess and splendour of the Prince, their conversation ending by Charlotte saying: " How I should like to meet so good and great a man."

Yvonne said nothing, but her thought was: " No one could be greater or better than Henri."

It was late when Henri left and the girls retired. Charlotte was feeling somewhat sad, she must part from Yvonne and set out on a perilous journey, not knowing what awaited her in the future. She felt sure her father's indignation would be terrific, and she might have to appear before an ecclesiastical tribunal to give an account of her actions, both in teaching the nuns Reformation doctrines and in breaking loose from the convent.

A woman of smaller disposition might have been tempted to feel jealous of Yvonne's happiness, but not so Charlotte; she loved Yvonne sufficiently to be genuinely glad that the love of a good man and the prospect of a happy marriage was hers, and she told Yvonne so with whole-hearted enthusiasm, as soon as they were alone.

Both girls were long in going to sleep that night: Yvonne was too happy for slumber and Charlotte too perplexed, but comfort came to her persently. As she prayed for help and guid-ance, a great calm took possession of her mind, and assurance of her Heavenly Father's love and that His presence would be with her; His power protecting; His strength sufficient for her. Faith triumphed over fear, and she felt that although the bit of the road she must travel now might be rough, yet presently she would find the green pastures and still-waters, so with quiet heart she fell asleep.

CHAPTER XXII

A SAFE JOURNEY

HENRI AND YVONNE were seated together in the rustic arbour in the corner of Jacques Baptiste's orchard. Spring was advancing and the apple trees were thick with blossom, pink and white. The birds were busy intent on nest-making, while they sung their joyous melodies. Love-making and happiness seemed in the air. In a distant field Yvonne could see Pierre Dupois and Nanette walking side by side.

Henri had been absent from the neighbourhood for some days, but he had managed to get a few hours' leave, in which he had ridden posthaste to the farm to tell Yvonne of what he had been doing. Now, as they sat together, he was speaking. " Only a week more, beloved, and then I have ten days' leave and we can be married. I have found a home for you, and my old nurse Denise is delighted at the idea of being with you; she is a dear old thing and you will love her, and I shall know she is taking care of you when I have to be absent."

" But Henri, will this horrible war cease soon, do you think ? It will be anxious work for me to have you away and in danger."

Henri laughed. " You mustn't worry, little one. You will be a soldier's wife and you will, I know, have courage. You have shown it in the past and you will again."

" Only as Christ strengthens me, Henri; but how I wish our land was at peace and there was religious freedom," Yvonne said.

" As it is in England," Henri replied.

" Oh, is it so in that land ? Tell me about it. I know so little of what is happening in other lands, or even in my own land, for that matter."

" I have English relatives," Henri told her. " My mother was an Englishwoman, and somewhere in the south of England, in a county called Somerset, I have cousins. They are Protestants, and the Queen of England is Protestant also. A short time ago there was persecution under a Roman Catholic queen, but now Protestants are able to confess their faith openly without fear of man."

" How glorious," Yvonne said. " How I should love to live there."

" Would you ? Perhaps some day I will take you there."

" Tell me about your mother, Henri."

" Ah, my mother ! Would she had lived to have known you, Yvonne ! She died when I was about nine, and my little baby sister died about the same time."

" Your little sister—why I remember her ! Do you recall a day when we were children playing in the Duchess's garden, and your baby sister was brought there by her nurse, and how fascinated Charlotte was with the baby ?

" Ye—es, I believe I do. It must have been soon after that that your father died."

" Poor Charlotte," Yvonne continued. " Once, in the convent, she broke down and sobbed bitterly because a baby who had been brought into the cloister garth by its mother clung round Charlotte's neck; she is so passionately fond of children. Henri, did you know that the Duchess had a conviction that some day Charlotte would be released from the bondage of Rome and become a wife and mother?"

" No. Did she really? Well, she has escaped from the convent, so maybe that is the first step in the fulfilment of the prophecy."

" I wonder how she has prospered on her journey. I do wish we could hear," Yvonne said. " She promised to let us know, if possible."

" Yes, but with the country in this disturbed state a messenger might be greatly delayed, even if Charlotte's brother-in-law was willing to send one."

Then Henri and Yvonne discussed their own affairs, Yvonne telling him some of the details of her life in the convent, and the wonderful blessing that had followed the reading of the Bible, and the Protestant literature that had reached them from an unknown source. She also told him of dear old Sister Marie Gabrielle and her triumphant death-bed. " Oh, how glorious is the Gospel," she said. " It brings peace to the soul, triumph in suffering, even in death."

" Yes, indeed. It is the Saviour Himself who enables us to triumph," So together they talked, rejoicing in all the good things God had given them.

Soon Henri's time was up, and together they strolled back to the farmhouse, happy both in the present and in anticipation of bliss to come when they should be united in marriage. Henri's last words were: " I have to go back to my post now, sweetheart; but in exactly seven days I shall be here to claim you for my own."

" If God wills it so, dear heart," Yvonne replied.

Henri held her in close embrace, murmuring: " Dearest, words fail to say what I feel toward you, my precious one," then he reluctantly turned away.

Yvonne stood in the doorway waving a farewell, and Henri, looking back, finally went off with a vision of the girlish form in the simple peasant frock framed in the dark opening of the door, with the sunlight glinting on her curly hair, for she had flung off her cap. Little did either dream of the sinister plot being made to destroy their happiness.

Meanwhile Charlotte and her companion had completed their journey. Through the mercy of God they had escaped detection. Sister Marie Agathe could act the peasant woman to perfection, and Charlotte left everything in her hands. It was with varied emotions that Charlotte at last drew near to the château of her brother-in-law, the Duke de Buoillon. Would she be welcomed there, or would Frances be afraid of offending her father if she received her sister?

However, it was useless to spend time in speculation as to what reception would be hers, she must go forward. Charlotte had written a letter which she meant to send in to her sister, for she felt sure that in peasant garb as she was, she would not easily gain admittance to the presence of the Duchess. Reaching the castle gate a harsh voice bade them be gone, but Charlotte's dignity, in spite of her clothing, made an impression on the porter as she stepped forward and spoke to him.

She told the man that she had come on an errand of utmost importance to the Duchess, and he allowed them to pass. They then traversed the long road to the drawbridge, and again they were permitted to pursue their way, and at last, after much delay, Charlotte's note reached the seneschal, who conveyed it to his mistress.

Charlotte's heart thumped noisily. She was weary and travel-soiled, and she longed for appreciation, home-comforts, and love. Would she be cast out now or . . .? But all doubts were set at rest as with a hasty rush her sister Frances came into the little waiting-room, and exclaimed: " Oh, Charlotte ! I have been so anxious about you—the news of your flight reached us through father, and I have been consumed with anxiety as to what had befallen you with the country in this disturbed state."

Frances embraced her sister warmly ; she was delighted to see her, for, as she afterwards told Charlotte, although the younger sister's memories of her elder sister were but faint, Frances cherished the recollections of the sweet baby Charlotte had been, and had always kept a warm spot for the little one in her heart, in spite of the fact that they had been separated for so many years.

Charlotte explained Sister Marie Agathe's presence, and Frances thanked the good woman for her faithful care. Soon Charlotte was seated in her sister's boudoir, dressed as befitted her rank, while Sister Marie Agathe was well cared for by the housekeeper.

Both Frances and Charlotte awaited the arrival of Frances' husband with a certain amount of wonder as to what he would say. For the moment he was absent. Meanwhile the sisters had much to tell one another. Charlotte describing her escape from the convent and her travels, and Frances telling of a visit she had recently received from their father. When Charlotte spoke of Henri de Valois' sudden appearance and his timely rescue from the brutal soldier, Frances interrupted: " We heard that Captain de Valois was involved with your flight, and now the authorities have placed a price upon his head—there is a reward to be given to anyone who can compass his death and produce evidence of it."

Charlotte started. " I am sorry to hear that. How terrible. But why should he be made to suffer for what is considered my misdeeds ? "

" Well, you must understand, Charlotte, that the Roman Catholics are furious at your action. You are accused of the inexpiable crime of instilling Lutheran doctrines into the minds of the nuns in your charge. You were an object of suspicion before your flight, and now, dear, both Robert and I are most anxious as to what will be the outcome of all this. The King is taking the matter up. Father is furious and will do nothing to help you, and anyone who assists or has assisted you is liable to punishment. I

M

think, too, Captain de Valois has proved such a stalwart partisan of the Huguenot cause, so brave in their defence, so clever in strategy, that the Roman Catholics are only too willing to jump at a pretence for making him an outlaw and tempting any ruffian to slay him."

" Oh dear! I was so delighted to have his assistance that evening, and to think he had met Yvonne at last; and now I wish he had been miles away, both for his own sake and Yvonne's.'

" Why Yvonne's sake? " Frances asked.

" I told you she escaped with me, and it is rather remarkable, but, years ago, when Henri and she were children, Henri promised to rescue Yvonne, and now it seems both have cherished the memory of each other, and so they are to marry ; they may even be married, for it s a month ago that I left them."

" Well, I can only hope Henri will escape. I wish he could be warned of his danger. We will see when Robert comes in if he can send a messenger with a letter. One thing, Yvonne's obscurity makes for her safety; every one's attention is focused on you and Henri."

" But Yvonne will suffer as much through Henri as if the danger were her own. I was so rejoicing that happiness had come to her at last, for the poor dear has had rather a sad life, and she is so sweet."

That evening Robert de la Marke, Duke de Bouillon, arrived, and soon Charlotte's tale was told to him. He welcomed her courteously as a Christian man and a relation, but it was evident that he felt anxious. He stroked his pointed

beard thoughtfully, and after a time of considera-
tion he spoke slowly and gravely.

" I fear, Sister Charlotte, you will be by no
means safe here. We shall not be able to keep
your presence a secret. I know the château is
being watched, and no doubt the arrival of two
strangers to-day has been already reported to
your enemies. But I have a suggestion to make.
My good friend Frederick, the Elector Palatine,
is a staunch Protestant and willing to befriend
all Huguenots. I think, without delay, we must
convey you to Heidelberg, the capital of the
Palatinate, where he has his residence. He and
his wife will, I am sure, welcome you, both
because of their friendship with us, and for a
deeper cause, that you are a child of God, whom
the Elector and Electress delight to serve."

Frances was sad at the thought of losing her
sister so soon, but she agreed with her husband
that Charlotte would be safer out of France, and
Charlotte left them to decide for her.

The Duke was almost inclined to make a
start with her at once, but finally resolved to get
a night's rest and be off with some trusted
retainers in the morning.

So once again Charlotte and Sister Marie
Agathe set out, and after a few days' journeying
reached the safe shelter of the Palatine's home,
to find rest and every kindness during their long
sojourn at the court.

CHAPTER XXIII

A DASTARDLY DEED

FRANÇOIS DROUET, the rough soldier who had been frustrated in his evil design on Charlotte and Yvonne by the timely intervention of Henri de Valois, was a man of vindictive disposition. Balked of his prey, he brooded over the incident until he had persuaded himself that he was a greatly injured man, and when it became known that a reward was offered to anyone who should slay Captain de Valois, François Drouet immediately conceived the idea of getting his revenge on the captain and earning the money at one and the same time. François called himself a good Catholic, inasmuch as he went to confession now and again and attended the ceremony of the celebration of the Holy Mass occasionally. He reckoned it a meritorious act when he had done a Huguenot a bad turn, and it by no means lessened his sense of satisfaction if by his action he benefited himself in any way. François' brain moved slowly, all the more so that it was often befuddled by heavy drinking; but he cogitated long, and as the result of his thinking he decided that he had no desire for an open struggle with the captain. François remembered only too well the blow he had received at the captain's hand on the eventful evening, but he fingered his carbine lovingly and visualised a swift shot from the covert of the bushes and thick undergrowth of the forest. Then the reward would be his, his desire for revenge would be satisfied, and he would have benefited the cause for which he was fighting.

François possessed a dogged kind of patience worthy of a less evil design, and once an idea had taken full possession of his mind he was not easily turned aside from his purpose.

The time passed and Yvonne was blissfully preparing for the day when Henri should come and claim her for his bride, while Henri was fully occupied with the many duties which came to him in his calling; he went happily about, all unaware of the evil purpose and constant watchfulness of the bad man who only waited for an auspicious moment to carry out his project. Time and again François was balked in his intention. He could not always find out where the captain was likely to be, for he had his own duties to perform; he hesitated as to whether he should seek a confederate, but the thought that if he did so it meant sharing the reward deterred him. François was greedy, and he longed to obtain the not inconsiderable sum entirely for himself. He began to grow desperate, the fear that someone else should do the deed while he waited for his opportunity made him furious—he knew there were many who were being tempted by the reward offered. Daily his impatience increased, and he often sought to calm his ruffled spirit, and at the same time keep up his courage, by long drinks at the tavern.

Then one day the longed-for chance literally dropped into his hands. He had been drinking, but not enough to make him indifferent to his objective, and when returning to camp in the dusk he espied coming toward him the figure he had shadowed for many a day; but not once had he been so near his prey, in such a solitary place, as at that moment.

" The saints be praised," François murmured, as he slipped behind some bushes and waited.

Henri, care-free and happy, approached the spot, whistling gaily as he strode along. Then a shot rang out on the evening calm; some birds, disturbed from the bushes, took flight; François staggered out from his hiding-place, and there on the rough woodland track, white and still, lay the one who only a moment before had been the embodiment of youth and health.

The perspiration broke out on François' face and he mopped his brow. Rough man as he was, the sight completely sobered him. He knelt beside the prostrate form for a moment and then said to himself: " Done for, sure enough. I must get help to carry the body to the authorities, for I must produce the proof of my deed or I shall not get the reward."

He glanced around, then decided that for the moment the body must be hidden or someone else chancing that way might forestall him and get the coveted bounty. So he dragged poor Henri into a ditch, covering him more or less with leaves, and then departed.

" I'm as dry as a bone," François murmured, as he went along. " 'Tis thirsty work, killing, but I must not linger to get a drink just yet."

Nevertheless when he drew near to the tavern

a boon companion was just about to enter, and, seeing François, invited him to come in and have a drink, promising to stand treat.

François hesitated but finally yielded, three reasons for complying coming into his mind. First, that the offer of a free drink was too great a chance to be refused, his grasping disposition could not resist that temptation; secondly, that had he declined his friend's invitation that friend would have wanted an explanation for such an unusual action; and thirdly, his thirst was too great to be ignored. So he went in, saying to himself: " Just one little drink."

However, liquor soon befuddled François' brain, and he quickly forgot what he had set out to do; one drink followed another, until before long he sank down on the sanded floor in a drunken slumber.

The next morning François awoke with an aching head. It was some minutes before he could recall what had taken place on the evening of the previous day. When he did remember, he hastened back to the scene of the encounter with the captain. He was filled with fear lest someone should have discovered the body and claimed the reward. He was furious with himself that he had let so many hours slip by before completing his task, but he hoped that he would find all as he left it, for it was indeed a lonely spot. It was some little while before he could locate the position: ditches there were many, woodland tracks diverging here and there, clumps of bushes exactly like the one in which he had hidden, but at last he found the place. Yes, here were the sign of trodden grass, broken twigs. He hurried into the ditch, but to his immense chagrin the body was gone. The fallen leaves were stained with blood, there were marks of footsteps in the mud, he could even discern the depression where the form had rested, but nothing else met his gaze.

François Drouet was almost mad with rage. It was as he had feared, doubtless someone else would demand the recompense that should have been his, which he had so justly earned. Returning to the tavern, he sought to forget his disappointment by indulging in a drunken orgy.

On the morning of the day on which Henri had promised to fetch his bride, taking her to a Huguenot pastor with whom he had made arrangements for the wedding ceremony, the family at the farm were stirring early. Nanette was excited, and yet at times a little inclined to be tearful at the thought of losing her dear Mademoiselle Yvonne.

Yvonne's hands trembled slightly as she attired herself in her new clothes which had been so carefully prepared by herself, Mère Baptiste, and Nanette. She wore a farthingale with a full-gathered skirt falling from it straight to the ground, her bodice was stiff and peaked, finished at the neck with a cambric collar made fan-shaped. She possessed no jewellery, but her bright happy face with its healthy colouring and her sparkling eyes needed no adornment. A home-made wicker basket contained a scanty supply of clothing; foresmocks, kerchiefs, body-stitchets, mufflers, sleeves, and biggins, while a cloak was ready for her outdoor wear.

Henri was expected early, and Brigette Baptiste had a meal ready for him. A savoury odour issued from the *pol-au-feu*, home-brewed ale, cheese, a dish of buttered eggs, and clap-bread were prepared. The latter was made of flour mixed with water, rolled into a ball, then flattened by a board till it was as thin as paper, placed on a hot iron and put on the hearth to bake, first one side, then turned, until both sides were brown.

Nanette fidgeted in and out while Yvonne watched from the window. Slowly the sun rose in the sky, higher and higher, and the spirits of the watching women sank lower and lower until evening fell and all agreed that although something had hindered Captain de Valois coming that day, no doubt he would be there on the morrow.

But, alas ! day succeeded day, and no sign, no message came from Henri. The colour faded from Yvonne's cheeks and at night her pillow was wet with tears. Her kind friends knew not how to comfort her, but could and did pray that true consolation might come to her from the One who says: " As one whom his mother comforteth so will I comfort thee."

Both Jacques and Brigette Baptiste feared the worst, but they forbore to speak of their apprehensions to the young people. They said nothing, not even when Jacques came in one evening and finding his wife alone, told her that Miller Fontaine had heard a report that a drunken soldier in a tavern had boasted that he had killed Captain de Valois.

The troops had now left the neighbourhood, although the wounded still occupied the convent, so there was no opportunity of finding out whether there was any foundation for the report or whether it was an idle boast.

" We must do our best for the poor maid," Mère Baptiste had said. " Truly, I shall be glad of her help and company when Nanette is married, for she does not disdain to put her hand to any kind of work."

" No, indeed. She certainly earns her board and keep," Jacques responded.

" Yes, but it is not the right kind of work for one like her—born in a different station to us."

" I shouldn't fret about that, wife, for Mademoiselle does not."

" That she doesn't. I never met anyone so gentle and humble. 'Tis truly the spirit of the Master seen in her."

CHAPTER XXIV

HARD PRESSED

THE Elector Palatine sought his wife's guest with a grave face. He had that morning received a messenger who had brought news that threatened the peace of Charlotte de Bourbon. She had been a guest at Prince Frederick's palace for some weeks, and was much enjoying the happy home life and freedom from religious restraint which was now her portion. Charlotte had openly joined the ranks of the Reformation party, and publicly abjured the Romish doctrines, and lived in hopes that, having left France, she was to be allowed to live her life in the way she considered consistent with her Protestant belief.

The Princess and Charlotte were sitting together when the Prince entered, and his wife called him to come and look at her new possession, a spinning-wheel, only just then invented to take the place of a distaff and spindle.

"Just look, Frederick," the Princess exclaimed, " isn't it splendid ? Charlotte and I were just saying we shall be able to prepare wool and flax for garments for the poor quite twice as quickly as we have been able to do it in the old way."

Prince Frederick smiled. Both women were so pleased with their treasure and looked so happy that he was loath to bring them disquieting news. He examined the mechanism of the spinning-

wheel and asked questions, but his wife quickly
became aware that his attention was forced, and
she asked: " What is the matter, Frederick ? Is
there anything wrong ? "

The Prince tried to evade her question, but it
was useless, the Princess pressed her inquiry,
and at last he said: " I shall have to tell you both,
so I suppose nothing is gained by delay. A
messenger arrived this morning to tell me that
Charlotte's presence here is known, and that the
President of the French Parliament has orders
to send an emissary to inquire into her position.
It seems that the President himself has been to
Jouarre to find out exactly what happened, and
how Charlotte took her flight. A price has been
put on the head of Captain de Valois, as it is
understood that without his aid there could
have been no escape. No trace can be found of
him. A rumour goes round that he has been
killed; others think he has fled somewhere for
safety—it may be to England, as I understand
numbers of Huguenots are doing, as the English
Government is giving them protection and aid.
But what we have to consider, dear," the Prince
continued, looking at his wife, " is what is best
to do for our young guest. Don't feel unduly
alarmed, Charlotte; as long as you remain here
I cannot but feel that the French King and
Parliament will have some respect for my
wishes."

Charlotte had turned white at the Elector's
words, and now she said, " Prince, I think my
father has something to do with this inquiry.
His intense hatred for Protestantism has led

him to influence the King against me, or rather it is not me personally but my religion that he hates. What can I do? I feel it so keenly that my own father is my enemy."

The Prince pondered, and then said, " I think the best thing I can do is to write a letter to your father explaining your position, and telling him that you are under my protection. Will you also write to him, and we can send our letters by this messenger, who will be setting out on his return journey to-morrow."

" Yes, I will. I will beg father for the sake of the love he bore me when I was a child to be reconciled; but I must make him understand that, although I am willing to yield obedience to him on every other matter, I cannot deny the truths I have learned, or give up my faith to please him."

" Then write your letter now, Charlotte, and I will prepare mine also, that the messenger may make a speedy return."

Charlotte wrote pleadingly, and tears fell now and again as she composed her letter. She longed to be reinstated in her father's home, but she felt that unless he promised his protection it was too dangerous to leave the shelter afforded her by the Prince. God had brought her to the court in a wondrous fashion, and she must not lightly run into danger.

Having finished her letter, she took it to the Princess to read, who approved of all she had written, and in due time the messenger was dispatched.

Many days elapsed before a reply came, and

then Charlotte, who had so longed for a favourable answer from her father, was disappointed. His letter was bitter indeed. He wrote that Charlotte had violated her promise to God, disgraced her family, and that he would never forgive her unless she returned to France with the intention of submitting herself to the orders of the King and the will of her father. Charlotte retired to her room when the Prince had read the Duke's letter to her. Her grief was so great that she shrank from even the kind words spoken by both the Prince and Princess. She must be alone, and although she had kept up bravely in the presence of her friends, in solitude her tears flowed. She had scarcely realised, until that moment, how much she had been hoping for a kindly letter from her father. For a long time she could only hide her face in her hands and sob. The tempter drew near, and whispered: " Is it worth while holding out against your father ? Here you are, dependent on the charity of others, while if you return and comply, at any rate outwardly, your father will be pleased, you will be in your own home, and doubtless before long a wealthy and suitable suitor will be found for you, so give in."

Charlotte was tempest-tossed; she flung herself on her knees by her couch and prayed, asking for strength, comfort, and guidance. As she prayed, she grew strong once again, and presently she sought the Prince, determined to make a suggestion to him. She knew that any decision she might make must be done quickly, as the messenger who had brought her father's letter would wish to return to his master without delay.

The Prince was amazed when Charlotte announced, " I am willing to return to my father if the King will become surety that I shall be allowed free exercise of my religion."

The Prince demurred, but Charlotte said, " I have prayed for guidance, and I feel if the King will give his promise, I shall take that as a sign that I am to return home."

" You have changed your mind, Charlotte; for only a short time ago you felt it would be rash to leave here, after God had so guided you to us," the Prince said.

" Yes, I know it looks like fickleness on my part, and yet I feel I must make this offer."

So the Prince forbore to say anything more, and accordingly wrote as Charlotte suggested, and again came a time of waiting; but when at last the Duke replied, he gave his daughter to understand that if she persisted in being a Protestant he would rather she remained in Germany—he would have nothing to do more with her.

Both the Prince and his wife hoped this would be the last communication they were to receive from France, and that Charlotte would now settle down among them; and doubtless, they said one to another, a suitor would be found for her hand before long. And the Princess, so happily married herself, could wish for nothing better for her young friend.

Charlotte was both relieved and disappointed; grieved at her father's final renouncement of her and yet glad that she was not called to face the ordeal of being thrown among Roman Catholics once again.

The days passed happily and busily, for the Princess was " full of good works which she did," and Charlotte aided her gladly. Then once again the even tenor of their lives was disturbed. An important deputation arrived at the castle. The King of France had sent two of his officers to interview the Elector and Charlotte with the intention of persuading Charlotte to recant. It was evident that had she been in France vengeance would swiftly have fallen on her, but the French King had no desire to seriously offend the Elector Palatine, Prince Frederick.

Persuasions and threats might be indulged in, but further than that the King, the Duke, or the Roman Catholic party did not venture.

Long dissertations followed the arrival of the deputation, for the two officers were well primed. Charlotte was sore pressed. Arguments, entreaties, promises were all brought to bear upon her. Her father's grief and disappointment at his child's behaviour were made the most of. A word-picture of his broken heart was cleverly given, and Charlotte was greatly moved, but ringing in her ears were the words: " He that loveth father or mother more than Me is not worthy of Me," and quietly but firmly she answered all their arguments, and at long last the two officers returned to their royal master nonplussed.

" Well," said one to the other as they wended their homeward way, " I am amazed that a woman should be proof against the inducements we offered: a place in the royal household; the recognition of the King himself; her father's favour; the prospect of marriage. But she refuses all, and prefers to be dependent on the charity of a foreigner. Well, well, women pass my understanding ! "

The other growled a reply, too disgusted almost for words at having to report that they— important as they considered themselves—had failed to persuade a woman to comply with the wishes of their master.

CHAPTER XXV

AN ANGEL IN HOMESPUN

A SICK man stirred uneasily on his humble couch. For many, many days he had been unconscious; now slowly his brain power was beginning to assert itself, but there was a feeling of great weariness, a strange unwillingness for either thought or movement. It was too much effort to open his eyes. Feebly he began to wonder what had happened to him. He had not strength to lift his head or move a finger, so he lay still, half-unconscious, glad of the sense of stillness all around him. Suddenly he caught the sound of gentle singing in a tone weak but musical; it was evidently the voice of someone who had possessed the gift of song in days of youth, but now grown old. The invalid found himself listening intently. Where could he be? he wondered. As the words rang out he murmured to himself, " It is someone accustomed to Huguenot gatherings." It soothed him to hear once again the precious words, in the singing of which he had often joined:

> My Shepherd is the Living Lord,
>   Nothing therefore can I need;
> In pasture fair, near pleasant streams,
>   He setteth me to feed.
>
> He shall convert and glad my soul,
>   And bring my mind in frame

To walk in paths of righteousness,
  For His most Holy Name.

Yea, though I walk the vale of death,
  Yet will I fear no ill :
Thy rod and staff will comfort me,
  And Thou art with me still.

Through all my life, Thy favour is
  Thus freely showed to me,
And in Thy House for evermore
  My dwelling-place shall be.
                            (STERNHOLD, 1562.)

The sick man drifted into an uneasy slumber
for a short time, and when he awoke once again
the words and tune still vibrated in his ears, and
for the moment he imagined himself present in a
gathering of simple, devout worshippers.

Presently, however, with what seemed to him
an immense effort, he opened his eyes and gazed
wonderingly around. He was lying on a low
bed in a room with rough rafters overhead and
a mud floor. His covering consisted of a home-
woven woollen rug, but his head rested on a
hand-spun linen cloth—it felt cool and pleasant
to his cheek. A big fire of logs burnt on the
hearth, before which lay, curled against one
another in great content, a huge shaggy dog and
a wee kitten. Strings of onions, dried herbs, and
some bacon hung from the rafters; the furniture
consisted of one or two benches and a table
composed of boards resting on trestles. An
opening in the wall served as a window through
which the summer breeze blew. The invalid

tried to raise himself on his elbow, but fell back with a groan.

As if in answer to that groan the door was pushed open and an elderly woman entered, dressed in simple peasant clothing. She stepped toward the bed, and when she saw her patient's eyes were opened and met hers with an inquiring gaze, she murmured, " Praise the Lord ! "

" Where am I ? " the sick man asked, and the woman answered, " You are in safe hands, Captain de Valois; so don't worry—just lie still and rest. No, no, don't move," she added, as he tried to raise himself. " Your wound has only just begun to heal, and I do not want you to start it bleeding again, just be a good lad, and leave everything to me till you are a bit stronger."

She placed her hand gently with a soothing movement on his brow, and Henri, looking up into her face, felt as though he had looked on the face of an angel, so full of loving-kindness and peace was it.

The next moment she had moved to the fireplace, and into a pot which hung suspended over the logs she dipped a mug, and then added a few spoonfuls of some liquid from a *marmite* that stood in the embers, and brought the mug to Henri.

" Now drink this broth; it is a strengthening mixture and has kept you alive so far, although it has been trouble enough to get it into you," she said with a smile.

Henri obediently drank, and as soon as he had finished his eyelids closed and he again slept, this time more peacefully, and his nurse, looking on, again murmured, " Praise the Lord; he'll do now, I'm thinking."

When next Henri woke it was evening, and he found the woman was sitting by the fire busy with her spindle and distaff, while on a bench opposite her sat a heavy-looking young man. He lay watching them, wondering who they were in a tired, hazy fashion, and as he watched the woman laid aside her work and, fetching two earthenware bowls from a shelf, she poured into them some savoury smelling broth from a *marmite* on the hearth, and the two had their evening meal.

Then the woman, speaking very slowly and distinctly, said, " It is time for you to get to bed, lad, but we'll have our evening prayer first."

Both knelt, and Henri de Valois closed his eyes and the tears slowly coursed down his cheeks, as he listened to the outpouring of the desires of the saintly dame under whose roof he found himself. She prayed for her country, for the King and Queen-mother, the persecuted Christians and all who were hard pressed because of their faith and allegiance to the truth as revealed in the Word of God; she prayed for the sick man whom she was nursing, and for herself and her son, for protection from their enemies if it were God's will, and if otherwise that they might have the grace to stand firm even unto death.

Henri de Valois was satisfied that he was in a Protestant Christian home; there was no crucifix, no use of rosary, no intercession to the Virgin

Mary, and in his weakened and prostrate condition the prayer moved him greatly.

Presently rising from their knees, the young man disappeared, saying " Good night " as he went, the only words Henri had heard from him.

Then the woman turned to the bed and was delighted to find Henri conscious and strong enough to make a few remarks.

" Ah, Captain," she said, " you have taken a turn for the better; we shall soon have you about again."

" How is it you know me, and how did I get here ? " Henri inquired.

" I know you because I have seen you at our Huguenot gatherings, and listened to your helpful words more than once; and how you came here I'll tell you sometime, but now I must dress your wounds and give you some food."

" It is very good of you to care for me like this," Henri said.

" What we do for the Master's servants is done unto Him, sir," she replied simply, and then busied herself attending to Henri's needs, after which she insisted on him composing himself for the night, promising to tell him what he wished to know in the morning.

CHAPTER XXVI

DAME BLANCHETTE'S STORY

NEXT morning the good woman pulled a stool to the bedside and settled herself down to answer Henri's questions.

" It was somewhere about a month ago that my son was out in the woods one evening with the dog. The animal became interested in something in a ditch, and my son thought he had got a rabbit. The dog scraped and whined, so Louis went to look, and found you, dead, he thought at first; but as he was not sure, he fetched me and I saw you were still alive, but that, unless you were attended to at once, it would soon be all up with you. My son is very strong—that is, strong physically, poor lad—so I directed him how to lift you, and together we brought you here. By the mercy of God, and in answer to my prayer, wisdom was given to me to know how to treat you. My father was reckoned a wise man, skilled in the use of herbs, and all he knew he taught me, so I have known as well as—perhaps better than—some of the leeches how to attend to you."

" But now, I wonder, did I get into that sorry plight ? " Henri asked with a puzzled frown.

" Why, sir, didn't you know there was a price on your head ? A reward offered which doubtless tempted some villain to kill you."

" No, indeed, I did not know; but why, I

wonder ? "

The dame could not help him as to the reason, and Henri felt puzzled. Memory of that fateful evening was coming back to him, and he recalled the sudden shock, but who had fired the musket he knew not.

" Has no one made any inquiry for me ? " Henri asked.

" We are very secluded here in the heart of the wood, sir. It is seldom anyone comes near us, and I felt it was wiser not to speak of your presence when I have been into the village. These are perilous days for all who are Protestants, as you know; so what with that and the special enmity that there seems to be against you, I kept quiet. I heard that it is rumoured that the troops have left the neighbourhood, so it may be that your friends think you have gone also."

" I must get up as soon as possible. I am greatly distressed to find that a month has elapsed since I was brought here. I—I——" he paused and a feeling of faintness made him lie back in a state of exhaustion.

The dame refused to allow him to talk any more then, but next day he told her of his engagement and how his absence must be causing suffering to Mademoiselle d'Arande.

" Could I send her a message ? " he asked; but Dame Blanchette did not know anyone who could be trusted with the knowledge of the Captain's presence there. The Baptistes' farm was some miles distant—too far for her to travel herself.

Henri naturally thought of the son as a

possible messenger, but the dame explained that he was half-witted.

"A good lad," she said. "Hard-working, but he never goes beyond these woods."

Henri sympathised, and the dame continued, "It is not often I speak of it, sir, but it was caused by shock I received as a young wife. My husband gave his life for the Truth; the priest denounced him to the authorities, and they killed him before my eyes, because he refused to recant and deny his Lord. The Master knows it was for His sake my man gave his life, and He will care for my boy. I am sometimes tempted to be anxious as to what will become of him if I am taken first, or what I shall do in my old age, but I know my Heavenly Father will care both for my lad and myself, so I do not fear."

"Even to your old age I am He; and even to hoar hairs will I carry you: I have made and I will bear; even I will carry, and will deliver you," Henri quoted softly.

"Ah," Dame Blanchette said with appreciation in her tone, "I heard those words once at one of our Huguenot gatherings, and I have wanted to hear them again. Do they come from God's Word?"

"Yes," Henri replied. "They are from the Book of Isaiah."

"How splendid it must be to be able to read the blessed Book; that has never been my privilege, but my husband could read a little and God has given me a good memory, so I am able to retain much of what I hear at the meetings," Dame Blanchette said.

" How old is your son ? " Henri asked.

" Turned thirty, sir; but he is like a child, always obedient to me, and wonderfully clever with animals. Our goats all know him, he can do anything with beasts of any kind; he seems to possess a soothing influence over them, but he shrinks from contact with human beings. He cannot talk much, although he can always make me understand all he wishes to tell me."

Henri was looking weary, and the good woman left him to rest; he was feeling troubled indeed at his inability to reach Yvonne, and his very anxiety retarded his progress. He was extremely weak from loss of blood, and some days he almost lost desire to live. Accustomed to good health, it was a new and trying experience for him to be helpless day after day. He was so obviously fretting, that one day his kind nurse spoke very plainly to him.

" Do you remember, sir, one day at one of our meetings speaking of trusting God in the darkness ? You told us that it was in the testing times, in the cloudy days, that we could prove our love for the Master by our trust in Him and in His dealings with us. Well, now you have the opportunity of living out your own words. God has spared your life for some purpose, I have no doubt, for it was a wonderful providence that my son found you when he did—an hour or two more of neglect and you must have died. Now He wants you to learn some lesson by this inactivity. Just ask Him to give you patience and make you an apt scholar, and trust your dear one into His keeping. He will not fail you in your need."

" Do pray for me and for her," Henri said, and Dame Blanchette there and then prayed by his side. Her earnest petitions and words of trust fell like balm on Henri's wounded, fretted, restless spirit, and from that day he was more peaceful, and consequently made progress in regaining strength. Before long he was able to sit by the fire, and soon take a few steps into the woods; dressed in the peasant clothing of Louis Blanchette, gaunt and feeble, no one would have recognised him as the erstwhile gallant, well-set-up soldier.

One day when he was beginning to think he would soon be able to traverse the miles to Jacques Baptiste's farm, Dame Blanchette came back with disquieting news from a visit she had paid to the village.

It was August 1572, and she brought the tidings of the massacre of St. Bartholomew. " Thousands of men, women, and children have been slain, they tell me, by the order of the King and his mother. The gendarmes are hunting out the Huguenots everywhere, especially around Paris."

Henri was anxious for more tidings than the dame could give. He thought of Admiral Coligny and his son-in-law M. Teligny, and longed to know more of them and others, so he determined to make the effort and get out into the world once again.

Dame Blanchette would fain have kept him until he was stronger, but she saw how eager he was, so could only pray for him and wish him God-speed.

" It will be well for you to go in these clothes,"
she remarked, as they sat together for the last
evening. " For one thing, your clothes were so
stained and torn and burnt, they would be of
little use, and Louis's garments make a good
disguise for you."

"'You think it wise for me to be disguised,"
Henri said.

" Yes, indeed. The man who fired at you may
be still about, and besides which you are known
as a Huguenot leader."

Henri departed next morning after trying, as
he had many times before, to thank the kind
woman who had saved his life. She refused to
accept the small sum of money which had been
found untouched in an inner pocket in Henri's
garments, making clear that robbery was not the
motive of assault.

Weary days of tramping followed, for Henri
could progress but slowly. However, at last the
longed-for spot came in sight.

Yvonne had almost given up hope of ever
hearing anything of Henri again. She went about
her daily task with a sweet, submissive sadness
that made both Brigette and Nanette Baptiste's
hearts ache for her. Not one word of rebellion,
not one murmur did they ever hear; but she
grew thin and pale, and they were very troubled
for her.

She and Nanette were busy in the garden
when a low growl from their dog made them
aware of an intruder. Both girls looked up
apprehensively. All Huguenots were living at
high tension, for tidings of many being slain for

their faith, even in the country districts, had reached them ; but they were relieved to see it was only one feeble, haggard-looking peasant approaching.

"A fugitive fleeing from the persecutors most likely. Maybe we shall be able to help him," Yvonne said to Nanette as they waited for the man to draw nearer.

The next moment the blood rushed to her cheeks, receding quickly, leaving her white and shaking.

Was it ? No—it could only be a passing fancy, and yet—there was something about the poor fellow that made her think of Henri. But how could there by any likeness between this weary, worn, travel-soiled, sick-looking peasant and the handsome, well-groomed soldier of past days ?

But all doubts were put to flight as he held out his hands and exclaimed, "Yvonne, don't you know me ? "

With a cry of joy Yvonne sprang forward, and in a moment she was held fast in Henri's arms, all the sadness and weariness of the past weeks forgotten in a tumult of ecstasy and joy.

CHAPTER XXVII

A GLAD REUNION

An old gentleman was walking up and down with slow and measured tread on the terrace in front of an ancient French château. There was much to please the eye in his surroundings. A magnificent peacock spread his gorgeous tail in the sunshine, inviting admiration; at the far end of the grey stone terrace, flights of steps decorated with beautiful stone vases and garden sculpture, led to well-kept flower-beds, where gaily coloured blooms vaunted their summer beauty; toward the left were quaintly clipped yew trees, while in the distance could be seen field after field of ripening corn. An old deerhound kept close by his master with drooping tail and bowed head as if sharing the depressed mood of his owner, but the old man seemed unconscious of all around him.

Presently—with a gentle coo—some white winged pigeons came fluttering near as if intent on attracting his attention. Then the old man paused in his walk and, speaking aloud, said, "Ah, pretty dears. Henri's pets. Would he were here to see them! Alas, alas! Who can say where my boy is? Fool and hot-headed I was to thrust him from me, and now what would I not give to know—just to know whether my boy is alive or dead. The suspense of no tidings is breaking my heart; methinks I could be at peace if I heard that my boy was at rest with his mother, sad though those tidings would make me; but this uncertainty——" He broke off as an old servant came in sight.

M. de Valois beckoned to him. Full well he knew that old Antoine would be only too delighted to hear anything his master might have to say about Henri, for Antoine grieved sorely that Henri had been banished from his home.

"Antoine," M. de Valois said, "I've had disquieting news this very day."

"Ah, master, I feared when I saw that messenger arrive, that he might bring sad tidings," said the old servant.

"Yes. He tells me that my son is missing and has been for some time. It seems that he assisted Mademoiselle de Bourbon, the young Abbess of Jouarre, of whom I told you, to escape, and a price has been put on his head, and whether he has been killed or not no one knows. Ah, my boy! My boy! How everything without him seems to me dust and ashes. Long have I tried to persuade myself that I acted rightly in spurning him, and loneliness has been my portion, and now, now—if he is dead——" The old gentleman could get no further—his voice broke.

"Nay, nay, master, it may be that the young Captain is in hiding and so is safe," Antoine ventured to say.

"If I only knew. Perchance he has escaped to his mother's people in England; but I can get no rest wondering what his fate has been."

"Could we not go to that place where he was last seen, sir? Could we not make inquiries?

Surely someone will be able to tell us something."

M. de Valois stood quietly thinking. After a moment or two he spoke with renewed energy. " Antoine, yours is a wise suggestion. We will go. We can start to-morrow and go to Jouarre. We must be cautious in our inquiries; we do not want to put Henri's enemies on his track. I will make preparations for our journey at once," and with a quick footstep M. de Valois entered the château.

On the morrow M. de Valois' coach drawn by four horses, necessary for pulling a cumbersome vehicle along the rough roads of that period, accompanied by Antoine, the coachman, and two postilions, rolled out of the grounds of the château. Clothing was gay in those days; a man's dress was rich and heavy. M. de Valois wore an outer coat of velvet of deep crimson, his short breeches were of satin, his sleeves slashed showing a lighter shade of silk than the deep pink of his inner coat, which coat was opened to reveal an elaborately embroidered shirt. His velvet cap was plumed, and as the coach itself was brilliantly painted and upholstered the whole affair made a gay splash of colour on the landscape. The trappings of the horses and the clothing of the postilions all added gaiety to the cavalcade. M. de Valois was likely to impress the peasants and simple country-folk wherever he travelled.

Antoine was no less excited than his master. It had been a weary waiting time for him in the absence of his young master. He had longed that father and son might be reconciled, and now to think that at last the father had decided to seek the boy whom he had vowed he would never speak to again. Alternate hopes and fears took possession of both old men. Would their search end only in the sad confirmation of their fears that Henri was dead, or would they find him somewhere, or, at any rate, gain some information concerning him?

The days of travel passed without special incidents, and at last they were in the neighbourhood of Jouarre. Many people were willing to talk about the battle, the breaking open of the convent, the flight of the Abbess, but no one volunteered information relating to Captain de Valois, and at first M. de Valois hesitated to ask.

At last in desperation he ventured, when resting and dining at a tavern, to say: " And what became of the young captain who aided the Abbess in her flight ? "

" Ah, that I can't say," replied the voluble innkeeper, who had so willingly talked. " There was a price on his head, and some say that he is dead, others say that he is in hiding; but if you really want to know, I have no doubt Baptiste the farmer might be able to tell you, for it was at his farm that the Lady Abbess and a young nun found shelter. They do say the nun is still there, but 'tis some miles from here and I have enough to do without visiting folk, and I don't happen to have seen Farmer Baptiste for many a long day."

M. de Valois changed the conversation; he did not want the innkeeper to think he was specially interested in the young captain. But he had taken note of the farmer's name, so it was not long before Antoine and he were wending their way to Farmer Baptiste's home. The horses were stabled and left in charge of the postilions at the nearest inn, and the two old men made their way on foot through the woods to the farm. Emerging from the forest into the open country, they hesitated which way to take, but presently espied a figure at work in the fields, so they went towards him intending to make an inquiry.

The man in the blue shirt and homespun breeches of a peasant saw them coming, and, as they drew near, his face, already pale and emaciated, turned ghastly, and he leaned hard on the handle of his implement to save himself from falling.

"My good fellow, can you direct us———" M. de Valois began, but he got no further, for, with a cry of mingled joy and dismay, Antoine rushed forward saying, "Monsieur Henri, Monsieur Henri!"

Henri's father gasped. Was Antoine mad? But no, on closer scrutiny he too saw that the man whom he was addressing, disguised as he was, looking wan and suffering, was nevertheless his son.

Henri still trembled. Had his father come as a friend or a foe? But soon all fears were allayed as M. de Valois took him by the hand and could scarce speak for emotion.

Together in the field they took counsel. Henri found his father full of sympathy, and overjoyed to think his son was alive and that he had now the opportunity of atoning for his harsh treatment in the past. There was much to tell, and when Henri almost hesitatingly spoke of Yvonne d'Arande—for he remembered the day long ago when as a boy he had spoken of his determination to marry her, and his father's opposition—what was his joy to hear M. de Valois say: " Ah, my boy, I have learned many a lesson in these years of solitude since last I saw your face, and I will not oppose your choice. But is there no place where we can go to make your plans, for you are unfit to stand talking here ? "

Henri suggested returning to his kind friends the Baptistes, but asked his father and Antoine to linger a little while outside the house while he made known their arrival to Yvonne.

Entering the house he found Yvonne alone, busily preparing the evening meal. She smiled sweetly at his appearance, and then said: " Henri, you look agitated. I do hope there is nothing wrong, no fresh trouble ? "

Henri laughed.

" Oh, ye of little faith. Did you not this morning tell me, dearest, that you had the conviction that guidance as to our next step would soon come ? And you were right. A wonderful thing has happened, and yet I should not say that, for it is what we have prayed for. You know how intensely I have longed for a reconciliation with my father—for some sign from him that he still cared for me ? "

" Oh, has he sent a message ? " Yvonne asked.

" Better than that, dear heart. He is here— and old Antoine of whom I have often told you."

Yvonne was amazed. " And is he friendly ? "

she asked.

" I should just think so. He has been yearning for me since his anger cooled, and at last he could bear the separation no longer and determined to seek me; but I must not keep him waiting—let me bring him in. "

Soon M. de Valois was introduced to Yvonne, and he told Henri afterwards that he fell in love with her on the spot.

" And now, my lad, I must think what is best to be done for you. It appears to me that for a time you and this little girl of yours had best find shelter in England."

England ! Yvonne flushed excitedly at the sound. England ! Where the good Protestant queen reigned and where she and Henri would be safe. Every day her loving heart had been tortured for fear Henri's foes would discover him—some bigoted Roman Catholic who would denounce him to the authority because of his faith, or some villain who for the reward offered would seek to take his life—and now if they could only reach the coast safely how glorious everything would be.

Henri agreed, a little sadly, for he loved his country and the old château, the home of his boyhood days.

" For a time, my boy, for a time only, we hope, we must make our home there."

" You too, Father ? " Henri asked.

" Yes. I cannot be separated from you for long, now I have found you. This is my idea : we will make our way to the coast—Boulogne, I think, will be the best town for our purpose. You can be disguised as one of my postilions; you can wear his livery and I shall send the lad home. We shall only linger at Boulogne long enough to get you two young people married, then when I have seen you safely on a vessel bound for England I shall return to the château, set my affairs in order, and join you in that land where we can dwell at peace. Does that suit you, my children ? "

A glance at the faces of both Henri and Yvonne satisfied M. de Valois; he saw that his suggestion met with their approval, but all Henri said at the moment was: " Father, this is good of you to exile yourself for our sakes."

" Tut, tut ! You want someone to look after you it seems to me—you are a bit of a scarecrow now."

Henri laughed, and Yvonne said: " Henri has not yet recovered from his serious illness—he very nearly died then."

" Yes, and I must seek out those good people whom you say nursed you so faithfully; they must be rewarded, and these also who have sheltered you here," M. de Valois said.

CHAPTER XXVIII

YVONNE'S FATHER-IN-LAW

PRESENTLY Jacques and Brigette Baptiste accompanied by Nanette returned and were amazed to find what visitors had arrived. M. de Valois was struck by their gentle courtesy; there was a quiet dignity about them, especially Brigette, that would have graced a duchess. He marvelled, and then thought: " I believe it has something to do with their religion. I have noticed this kind of thing in Huguenots before."

That last evening at the farm was a time of mixed feelings. The Baptistes were in a measure relieved to find their guests were provided for, as they had been anxious as to what might at any time befall them, and yet they were sad at saying " good-bye," especially Nanette, who oved Yvonne dearly; but Pierre came in later and did his best to cheer her, while both Henri and Yvonne promised that when the time should come that it was safe for them to return to France, one of the first places they would visit would be the household that had so nobly given them succour in time of need.

M. de Valois was able to give Henri some of the sad and terrible details of the massacre of St. Bartholomew. He reported that about five hundred noblemen and ten thousand persons of inferior rank had been slain. " Do you wonder," said Henri's father, " that I am anxious to get you out of this land, so dangerous for all who profess your faith? "

" Ought I to desert those who are left? " Henri said musingly, but both his father and Yvonne pointed out to him that in his weakened condition he could be of no use; at any rate for the present, rest and care were needful for him.

" It almost seems as if nearly all have perished," Yvonne said sadly, but Henri assured her that such was not the case. He knew the strength of the movement, and felt sure that there were many thousands still left in France to uplift the banner of truth, Protestantism, and Christ in spite of the efforts of CharlesIX and his mother, Catharine de Medici, to exterminate the Huguenots at one blow. Henri asked for still more information; in the backwater in which he had been for weeks he had hungered for tidings.

So M. de Valois continued—explaining details for the sake of the Baptistes—" Admiral Coligny, that brave general who had the title of admiral conferred on him by HenryII (father of our present King) as a reward for his bravery in the wars of Spain, has been killed. He was stabbed in his bedroom and his body thrown out of the window."

Henri was overcome with emotion at this news, for he had known and loved Admiral Coligny.

"Ah," he said, " if only Coligny's efforts to found a colony in Florida to provide a safe shelter for Huguenots had succeeded, what suffering it might have saved; but the settlers who went there ten years ago were all slain by the Spaniards. But, tell me, Father, did our young King approve of this horrible massacre? I had hoped better things of him."

" My son, you know what he is, a puppet in his mother's hands. Poor young man! His tutor, Maréchal de Retz, made it his business to stifle all tendency to good in the young King, to teach him to swear and deceive. I am told that on the fateful day of the massacre he was in a state of great agitation, trembling from head to foot, and his mother and the Duke of Anjou had great difficulty in getting him to give the signal for the attack, the ringing of the great bell over the palace. It was not until past midnight that his bad advisers succeeded in persuading him to give orders that the bell should be rung, and even then Charles insisted that the life of his old nurse whom he loves, and also of his surgeon, both Huguenots, should be spared."

" If only he had spared Coligny," Henri said. " They have slain the best man in France; he was a saint indeed; not even his enemies could find any fault in him; heresy was the only crime of which they could accuse him."

" It reminds me of the story of Daniel," Yvonne said.

But it was getting late and M. de Valois rose at last to go, promising to be there in good time in the morning to start on the jounrey. All were up by dawn the next day, and soon the travellers were off. M. de Valois intimated that he should visit the farm again on his way back to his home, as he wished for a talk with Farmer Baptiste.

The old gentleman had managed to provide,

for Yvonne's comfort in travelling, a pelisse and hood so elegant that Yvonne flushed with pleasure. Never had she expected to wear anything so pretty, and at the same time so comfortable. The pelisse, made of velvet, had a collar of fur, and hung in long full folds fastened down the front with little buttons, so completely covering her simple, homely gown. Henri rode on one of the horses in the postilion's livery.

Yvonne felt somewhat awed when she found herself alone in the coach with her future father-in-law, but with extreme courtesy the old gentleman set her at ease, and presently to her joy she found he was able to give her news of Charlotte.

" The Duke de Montpensier is a neighbour of mine," he said, " and from him I have heard much of his daughter; she is now at the court of the Elector Palatine, and I think she is likely to remain there."

" Is he a Protestant ? " Yvonne inquired.

" Yes, my dear, he is," M. de Valois replied, and then he proceeded to tell Yvonne of Charlotte's stand for Protestantism and her father's rage.

" He is flinging himself with mad hate into this persecution of the Huguenots," M. de Valois said.

" I am sorry. Poor Charlotte, how sad it must make her feel ! "

" Yes, indeed." Then to Yvonne's surprise the old gentleman added: " I call myself a Roman Catholic, but—but—I have had many thoughts the last few years of my life, and I—well—I can hardly explain what I feel, but I

218 BEHIND CONVENT WALLS

want you and Henri to teach me the Truth as you understand it, if I'm not too old to learn."

Yvonne's eyes dimmed with tears; she felt the goodness of God surrounded her. She and Henri had trusted their Heavenly Father to undertake for them, and now their prayers were being answered and their trust rewarded a thousandfold.

M. de Valois asked many questions about the Baptistes. He was anxious that they should be recompensed for their kindness.

" Does he own his farm ? " he queried.

" No. He rents it from the convent authorities, and he is greatly surprised that he has not had notice to leave ere this. It is a daily anxiety to them, for they have heard a rumour that, owing to their failure to attend mass and go to confession, they are likely to be evicted."

M. de Valois was thoughtful. Presently he said: " It may be that I have come on the scene at the right moment. On my return journey I shall have a suggestion to make to these good people."

Yvonne asked no questions, but she was delighted that the Baptistes were likely to be relieved from their anxiety and rewarded for their goodness.

CHAPTER XXIX

A LITTLE group of horsemen were wending their way to Heidelberg. At their head rode William of Nassau, Prince of Orange, known as William the Silent; the Prince whom Charlotte de Bourbon had long before expressed a desire to see. He rode somewhat wearily, for life had dealt him many a hard blow, and he was now on his way to the court of the Elector Palatine to take counsel with that good Protestant Prince.

At the age of eleven William had succeeded to great possessions left him by a cousin who had died childless, and he had been sent from his father's home in the Netherlands to be educated in a foreign court; but although away from home influence and a page at a court where history was being made daily, and where it seemed likely that young William would easily drift into a life of luxury and magnificence, varied, it may be, by military adventures, yet the early training of his good mother was not lost. Juliana of Stolberg was a woman of fine character and sincere piety. She had five sons and seven daughters, and she not only taught them Protestant truths, but as they went out into the world she kept in touch with them by her letters, writing simple, earnest counsel, as if they were still her little children; and in all the dangers they encountered she begged them still to rely on the guiding hand of God. It was doubtless owing to that mother's influence that William took such a stand for Protestantism and suffered the loss of wealth, lands, and much besides, in order to lay the foundations of a free Protestant commonwealth in the Netherlands, where persecution had been terrible, many thousands having perished by the command of the King of Spain. Prosperous towns had become almost depopulated, grass grew in the streets where once cheerful citizens had carried on useful trades.

The name " Silent " was given to William not because he was of a taciturn disposition—on the contrary, he was possessed of a fluent, agreeable tongue and a gracious manner, and was a delightful companion; but he won the title because of his great discretion in receiving silently an important communication from Henry of France. The French monarch and William found themselves alone together one day when hunting, and, the king's mind being full of the scheme which had been formed by Philip of Spain and himself to extirpate Protestantism in France and the Netherlands by slaying all Protestants, the French king spoke freely of this plan to William, who, although dismayed and indignant, kept silent, and the king had no idea of the blunder he had committed.

Many years had passed and much warfare taken place between that day in the forest and the day when William rode to the Palatine court, where Charlotte had been living for three years.

He had been married twice, first to Anne of
Egmont, which venture in matrimony had proved
exceedingly fortunate, although the young couple
were only eighteen years of age at the time of
their marriage. That period of happiness only
lasted seven years, during which time William,
being a wealthy man and very hospitable, enter-
tained largely; not only the noble but men
of low degree were welcome at his table. His
second marriage, one of convenience for political
reasons, was a failure. Anna of Saxony was a
woman sadly unfitted by temperament and
intellect to be the wife of so great a man, and
William, who loved home-life and needed sorely
in the many hardships he endured as a soldier
the kindly support of a good woman, missed what
he had enjoyed in his first wife, only too sadly.

William, and his no less noble brothers, fought
and lost over and over again; their money was
poured forth, their lives risked on behalf of the
Netherlands, but they still persevered. Now, as
William and a few of his faithful followers
wended their way to the Palatine court, William
was reminded that he would meet there the late
Lady Abbess of Jouarre. William had long taken
an interest in her extraordinary story and had
desired an interview with her. He felt that she
must be a woman of both sterling character and
great faith, and now at last his wish to know her
was to be gratified.

After an important interview with Prince
Frederick, the Elector Palatine, himself a home-
lover, introduced Prince William to the ladies,
the Princess and Charlotte. William was charmed

with Charlotte. Her gentleness and intrepidity, so happily blended in her character, captivated him. Long a wanderer and a warrior, he craved for a haven made for him by a good woman's presence and love.

His stay at the court was not long at that time, but he soon found his way back again and sought Charlotte.

The Princess, woman-like, took a keen interest in the wooing, and arranged that William should seek Charlotte in the garden, where he told her of his love.

Charlotte was convinced that this was God's will for her, His plan for her life. She had firmly believed that her mother's prophecy would be fulfilled, since she herself had learned to know the Saviour and had received faith to trust in His overruling Power. She had been only waiting until God sent the one to whom she could give her love and confidence and to whom she might devote her life.

They were an unusual couple. William was at that time forty-two, but looked older as the result of the strenuous life of warfare and intrigue which he had lived for many years, and Charlotte was twenty-eight, she, whose life had been such a tremendous contrast to his, knowing so little of the world, of its politics or war. It seemed like the mating of an eagle and a dove.

" And you are willing, dear heart, to trust yourself to me, to share my life-work with all its peril and privations," William said.

" I believe," Charlotte replied steadfastly, with her characteristic composure, " I believe my life has been redeemed from its monastic bondage for that purpose."

Then William told her how at first his desire to help Protestants had not arisen so much from religious sentiment as a determination to protect a multitude of harmless men and women from a horrible fate, because his whole soul had re-belled against those wholesale murders, but latterly his mother's gentle wise teaching was beginning to bear fruit in a real faith in Christ for himself.

William was so much in love that he would fain have arranged a wedding ceremony without delay. Neither he nor Charlotte had any desire for a great show. William remembered with distaste the extravagant display, the days of feasting, the pageantry at his wedding with Anna of Saxony, and recalled the bitter dis-appointment that followed so swiftly, when Anna had given way to fits of ungovernable rage and petty jealousies. Now he only longed to get the rite of marriage performed as simply as possible and take Charlotte to his home in Antwerp; but, alas ! when they consulted the Elector Palatine they found things would not be as easy as they desired and hoped for.

" Delighted as I am to welcome you as a suitor for Charlotte's hand," the Elector said, " yet I feel I must point out to you that neither of you are ordinary citizens. Your high rank brings its responsibility, and for the sake of the nations you represent and for political reasons we must obtain the consent of both Charlotte's father and the King of France, if possible."

The faces of the lovers fell, but they saw the wisdom of their friend's remarks and agreed to wait until the Elector had written to both the king and the Duke de Montpensier and got their replies.

With mixed feelings Charlotte watched the Prince of Orange ride away. Joy mingled with grief. Joy that the love of so good a man was hers, and grief that he must go forth to a life of peril, which at the moment she might not share.

The days passed slowly. All people, lovers included, had to practise patience in those times, for there was no daily post, but at long last a messenger arrived bearing the all-important answers to the Elector's letters.

Prince Frederick sought Charlotte and read aloud to her the communications he had received. After the usual polite opening remarks the letter from the King of France continued: " The King will in no way compromise himself in all this, as it is against his religion, but the French court will not openly object to whatever Mademoiselle de Bourbon should do by the advice of the Elector Palatine."

The Duke de Montpensier's letter was not quite so favourable; he raised scruples, and yet it was evident there was an undercurrent of satisfaction that his daughter should be sought in marriage by so great a personage as the Prince of Orange. Charlotte thought that she detected a softening toward her—the letter certainly was moderate, very different from his former ones, which had contained such expressions of anger. So the Elector wrote once again begging the Duke to reconsider the matter. All were hopeful of an ultimate consent, for it seemed that the Duke was almost willing for the union and yet his pride did not permit him giving an immediate approval.

The waiting time came to an end. The Duke not only gave his consent to the marriage, but intimated that his daughter was not to be a penniless bride, a suitable dowry was forthcoming; and on 12th June 1575 the wedding took place, and Charlotte from that day devoted herself to the making of a happy home for the man whose public life was so full of hardship and peril.

CHAPTER XXX

TWO HAPPY WOMEN

" Oh, Henri, I am so excited ! To think that we are really going to see Charlotte at last, after all these years. Just exactly how long is it since we were separated at Jouarre?"So spoke Yvonne to her husband one day when they had been married some six years.

Henri smiled. Yvonne was not good at dates, and he knew her method of reckoning. Besides, happy days passed uncounted, and Yvonne had had six years of great joy.

" Let me see," she continued, " it was in the spring of 1572 that Charlotte and I escaped from the convent, and you and I were married in the September of that year. Then the treaty was signed on 6th July 1573. How delighted we were to get back here, Henri, to our own country. Of course, I shall never cease to feel I owe a debt of gratitude to England for sheltering us in time of peril, and your relations were so good to us, but, after all, one's own land must always be dear to one's heart."

" Yes, indeed I feel the same, but many of our countrymen seem to be content to remain in England, and I cannot but think England benefits—they are the best of our people and are teaching the English their trades and methods of industry. France has lost some of her most worthy sons."

" But, Henri, we must remember many of them had lost all they possessed, during the persecution; they had not a lovely place like this to which to return. But I was calculating how long it was since I saw Charlotte and you have put me off the scent."

Henri again laughed. " Try again, dear heart. You had got to the year of the treaty."

" Yes, and Charlotte married in 1575, and now she has two little daughters and it is the year of our Lord 1578, so it is———" Yvonne paused, counting on her fingers, and Henri laughed loudly.

" I've got it. Over six years since we met. I wonder if we have both changed much."

Henri looked at his wife with lovelight shining in his eyes. The years of happiness had not been without effect on Yvonne. Her cheeks were rosy, her eyes bright, the wistful, somewhat frightened look had entirely disappeared—it was easy to see she was a happy woman. She had grown a little plump, but she still had a girlish appearance for her twenty-five years; to her husband she was the personification of beauty and grace.

" I am longing to see Charlotte's babies. My only disappointment is that I cannot take my wee Aimeé to show to Charlotte, but she is too small for such a journey. Ah, here comes nurse with her."

An elderly woman came across the garden to the arbour in which Henri and Yvonne were sitting, bearing in her arms a little girl of some eighteen months, who nearly wriggled out of her nurse's arms with delight at the sight of her parents, and in her eagerness to teach them.

Henri rose at their approach and, pulling a garden chair near, bade the nurse be seated. He was always courteous to all his employees, and specially so to Dame Blanchette, who had saved his life by her skilful nursing and succoured him for so many weeks in her woodland hut.

Her son Louis was now dead, and Henri and Yvonne were only too delighted to give the good old woman a home. She was not allowed to work, although she superintended all the nursery regime, and was devoted to baby Aimée.

After playing a little while with their baby daughter, Henri and Yvonne returned to the château, talking together of their proposed trip to Antwerp to visit Charlotte.

" I shall not want to be away long from baby, Henri. In spite of the fact that she will be well cared for, yet I shall be anxious," Yvonne said.

" No need for that," Henri replied. " Never was anyone more faithfully served than we are. Dame Blanchette and old Antoine in the home, Père and Mère Baptiste on the home-farm, Nanette and Pierre not far off—we are surrounded not by servants, but by friends."

" Yes, indeed. It was lovely that your father was able to provide for Brigette and Jacques just at the time when the convent authorities had planned to evict them summarily, and it means so much to me to have Nanette near at hand. Pierre makes such an excellent woodman, too."

Entering the château they found M. de Valois sitting in the hall. He put down his book, and said: " Have you made your final arrangements for your journey ? "

"Yes, Father, we start to-morrow morning."

" Well, well ! I must not complain. I have you both with me most of the time, but do not be away too long. I never expected to be as happy as I am now. I have my son, my daughter, and my sweet grandchild to give me joy; but chief of all I find my greatest joy in this, and in the knowledge it has brought to me of sin forgiven and acceptance with God through the merit of our Lord and Saviour Jesus Christ."

The old man lifted the book he had been reading, and Henri and Yvonne saw that it was a copy of the Holy Scriptures.

"Thank God," Henri said, and Yvonne's eyes filled with happy tears. It was the first time M. de Valois had made definite confession of faith in Christ, although both his children had long felt that he knew the Lord as his own Saviour, but it caused them to rejoice that he was now able to speak openly of having received the gift of salvation.

In a few days' time Henri and Yvonne were at the home of the Prince and Princess of Orange. Charlotte, looking very matronly, with motherly pride showed her daughters, Louise Juliana, the first-born, and wee Elizabeth, the second.

"We called her Elizabeth after the English Queen, who has kindly consented to be her godmother," Charlotte told them.

When the little ones had returned to the nursery Charlotte and her friends settled down for a long talk.

Charlotte congratulated Henri on being able to return to his old home, and said: " Your sojourn in England was but brief, was it not ? "

" Yes, less than twelve months. The Roman Catholics found our party so vigorous and our defence at the siege of Rochelle so good, that the Duke of Anjou found it expedient to negotiate with us, and a treaty was signed, so we have peace at last, at any rate for the present."

" What a terrible thing the massacre of St. Bartholomew was," Charlotte continued. " Had I been in France then, I doubt if I should have escaped."

" Yours was a wonderful deliverance," Henri said, " and mine too, for at that time I was lying ill in Dame Blanchette's hut and no one knew where I was or that I was alive. Did you hear, Charlotte, of the remorse of the king before his death. His old nurse, who was a Christian woman and who owed her life to his protection, was with him. He spent his last days in groans and in tears, often exclaiming: ' What blood; what murders. Ah, I have followed wicked counsel. Oh, my God, forgive me, have mercy upon me if Thou wilt.' "

" He, who responded to the cry of the dying thief, doubtless heard his cry," said Charlotte, " but oh, the suffering he caused ! "

" And what about your father ? " Yvonne asked. " Is he reconciled to you now, dearest."

Charlotte shook her head sorrowfully.

"Not entirely, Yvonne. He tolerated my marriage and provided me with a dowry, but he has more or less ignored me since, although I think he is pleased that the Queen of England is friendly to us. I can only go on praying for him."

"Tell me about Sister Marie Agathe; she has passed over to the 'Other Side,' I understand," Yvonne said.

And Charlotte told her of the happy home-going of the good woman who had stood by Charlotte for so long, then their conversation drifted back to their childhood days, and they spoke of the good Duchess who had taught all three of them the Truth.

"Doubtless," said Henri, "we owe much to her prayers for us."

"Yes, indeed. When she passed away how hopeless our lives looked, and now here we are, delivered from the bondage of Rome and our prison, free to serve God according to His Book and the dictates of our consciences. And whoever could have dreamt, Yvonne, that you and I would be happy wives and mothers? It sometimes seems too wonderful to be true. Occasionally in my first waking moments, even now, I fancy I have dreamt it all and that I shall find myself back in that little whitewashed cell in the Convent of Jouarre, and then when I realise that it is true that I am a free woman, I am overcome with joy and can only praise God for all He has done for me."

"I need not ask if you are a happy woman, Charlotte, dear heart," Yvonne said, glancing at her friend's joyous countenance.

Before Charlotte could reply a hearty voice was heard, and someone exclaimed: " Who is asking if my wife is happy ? "

The curtain over the doorway was flung aside and in the next moment Charlotte had rushed to meet the newcomer.

"Oh, William ! I hardly dare let myself expect you home to-day. I am delighted ! Let me introduce my very dear old friends, Henri and Yvonne."

William welcomed his guests warmly, and said: " If only you knew the many times Charlotte has told me of the excellencies and virtues of you two, you would not be surprised to know I have longed to see you both, especially to thank you for the aid you gave my dear wife in escaping from behind convent walls."

Printed in the United States
64257LVS00004B/130-249